7- 8-

BEGUILING THE BARON

ELIZABETH KEYSIAN

SOUL MATE PUBLISHING

New York

BEGUILING THE BARON

Copyright©2019

ELIZABETH KEYSIAN

Cover Design by Syneca Featherstone

Published in the United States of America by
Soul Mate Publishing
P.O. Box 24
Macedon, New York, 14502

ISBN: 978-1-68291-963-7

ebook ISBN: 978-1-68291-877-7

www.SoulMatePublishing.com

I dedicate this book to

two inspirational teachers at

Chelmsford County High School for Girls,

Mrs. Jean Greenwood and Mrs. Mackrill.

Elizabeth Keysian is the monster you created, ladies.

Thank you so much for doing so.

Acknowledgments

I am extremely grateful to Char Chaffin, my fantastic editor, for her encouragement and professionalism. Thanks also to the rest of the team at Soul Mate Publishing—I'm thrilled to be one of their authors. I'm eternally grateful to my long-suffering partner, Tim Robey, and the two very special author friends I met early on in my writing journey, Anna Albo and Shelley Iñón. Thank you so much for having faith in me! I'd like to make special mention of Eve Pendle, a fellow British author who has helped me improve and fine-tune my writing— thanks Eve! If you haven't yet bought any of her books, I'd strongly encourage you to do so.

I would also like to extend my heart-felt thanks to two fantastic writers of romance, Barbara Monajem and Ingrid Hahn, who beta read this book for me. Again, if you haven't read their works, Dear Reader, you are seriously missing out.

Prologue

Selbury Poorhouse, Wiltshire, England
Maundy Thursday, 1822

The room was silent but for the breaths of childish concentration as Miss Galatea Wyndham's pupils bent over their mending. It was a struggle to see in the poor light admitted by the small, high window, and Tia feared the sorry creatures would all have headaches by the end of the morning.

What the poorhouse child needed was sunlight, exercise, fresh air—

"Letter for you, Wyndham." The beadle's harsh voice broke the stillness as he thrust open the iron door and pushed the folded piece of paper at her. A letter? Her young pupils were forgotten as Tia turned it over in trembling fingers and saw the seal of the Duke of Finchingfield on the back.

It had been broken, of course. The governor of the poorhouse had a great suspicion of letters. They made the inmates feel important, singling them out from the rest of the throng and giving them ideas above their station.

There was another reason, even less justifiable: that Tia and her mama were gentlewomen, far more likely to receive money by post than anyone else. The beadle and governor didn't approve of inmates being sent money either.

It was usually confiscated.

As she unfolded the missive, Tia prayed her friend Lucy Cranborne, now Duchess of Finchingfield, wouldn't have been foolish enough to enclose any banknotes or drafts.

Besides, even if she sent enough for the Wyndhams to buy themselves out of the poorhouse, where would they go? The sinking of Papa's one remaining ship, with him on board, had left his family with so many bills, they were equally as likely to find themselves in debtors' prison, once their creditors caught up with them.

At least for now, their creditors knew there was no point in hounding them while they were in the poorhouse.

My dearest Tia, Lucy had written, *I will send you no coin, for fear of it getting lost.*

Tia let out a sigh of relief. Clever Lucy knew better than to trust the authorities. Or, indeed, the post.

I know better than to offer you and your mama charity directly.

True enough. Mrs. Sarah Wyndham, though failing in health since her beloved husband's death, was too proud to accept handouts. She clung to the hope that a wealthy, distant relative to whom she had written would, at any moment, descend upon Selbury Poorhouse and whisk herself and Tia away to a palatial establishment in the country.

Tia wrinkled her nose. The odor of overcooked cabbage had invaded the sewing room—or cell, as she preferred to call it. A watery stew was being prepared to accompany the paupers' lunchtime dole of bread, and she heard the children's stomachs rumbling in anticipation.

Oh, for the smell of freshly cooked, butter-basted chicken, the comforting scent of a raised pie, the mouth-watering perfume of biscuits flavored with rosewater . . .

She shook away the memories. It was too distressing to ponder what she used to have. She needed to think about the present.

I have discovered a distant relative of yours, the letter went on, *and have appealed to him to assist you. I can see no reason he should not. He is a widower, though yet young, keeps very much to himself, and has a vast former religious estate in dire need of a woman's touch. You and your mama would be the perfect companions for him and for his daughter, Miss Mary (Polly) Pelham, who, by my reckoning is aged about nine. I know how you love children.*

Tia laid the letter in her lap, her eyes too blurred with tears to continue reading. It had come at last. They were to be freed from this institution, more like a prison than a home. Though she could do much good here, particularly amongst the largely illiterate children, it would be infinitely preferable not to be an inmate herself. She scarcely dared hope, after so many miserable, cold, dark and comfortless months, that escape was truly at hand.

Dashing the tears from her eyes, she checked the children were still absorbed in their tunic-mending and the darning of stockings. It wasn't unknown for frustration to get the better of them from time to time and if she was not watching, a little girl might pull off another's cap for a joke and be stabbed with a needle in reprisal.

All seemed calm, so Tia returned to the letter that fluttered in her unsteady hands. A nine-year-old girl for company. The same age her sister Phoebe had been when the putrid sore throat had cut short her life.

If all of this were to come to fruition, if Polly Pelham's father were to take them, Tia vowed she'd love Polly like a sister, or even a daughter. At one-and-twenty, she was more than old enough to have begun a family of her own.

But who exactly was Polly Pelham's father? She'd heard the surname somewhere before, but could not recollect where, or when. She scanned the letter, and her eyes snagged on a name.

Her blood ran cold. Henry Pelham, eighth Baron Ansford.

The man some believed to have murdered his wife.

Chapter 1

Henry Pelham gripped the battlements on the top of his folly tower and fought against the nausea that assailed him. His knuckles whitened as he stared down, out-facing his demons as he had done every day for the past three years, unable to forget the sound of the falling body striking the rocks below.

The wind tossed his long hair about his shoulders, and he gritted his teeth against the pelting rain, using the sting of it to stiffen his resolve, his own misery restitution for what his wife, the late Lady Mary Ansford, had suffered at his hands.

Lifting his head and scanning the grounds of his medieval home, Foxleaze Abbey, Hal knew again the bitter defeat of her loss, the guilt of being left with a motherless child, and the shame of being held responsible for a tragedy whose repercussions had changed the course of his life forever.

"My heart is dead," he told the pitiless spirit that haunted his every thought. "I live only to create a fitting memorial to you, Mary, and to make sure Polly is strong enough to withstand the censures of Society."

This dictum, repeated each day as part of his penance, calmed him with its familiarity. Hal turned away, duty done, and stepped down into the body of the folly tower, out of the storm.

The nausea was so intense, he could almost imagine the tower swayed in the wind, and he had to clutch at the rail as he made his way down the spiral staircase to the uppermost chamber, where a sputtering horn lantern did little to dispel the gloom.

"Foul weather for spring," he muttered to the restless spirit that dwelt there. "I'd not have them come while the roads are so rough. The month of May will be soon enough if they are to come at all."

Mary's shade gave him no answer, but he knew, deep in the worthy corner of what remained of his heart, he'd accept the Wyndhams into his home. He neither needed nor wanted the company of these distant relations, but Polly needed them, and if he did the right thing by Polly, perhaps, finally, the memory of his dead wife would stop tormenting him.

Somewhere beneath all the self-loathing, the black melancholy of his soul, he'd been surprised to discover a nugget of kindness lurking. Kindness had once motivated his political career, had been the guiding star of his universe, even though Mary had mocked him for it and told him it made him soft. His political adversaries would have called him anything but, though he doubted any of his stubborn determination to champion the oppressed remained.

Even so, there had been enough generosity in his heart to extend a helping hand to his destitute cousins. They'd suffered grief of their own and needed the charity he was able to give.

One of his few remaining friends, William Cranborne, Duke of Finchingfield, had used his skill with words to broker a deal between the two parties. Knowing Mrs. Sarah Wyndham to be a proud woman, the duke had promised to make sure she knew Hal wasn't offering a handout, but employment. In exchange for this employment, they'd have a sizeable allowance, food, clothing, and a decent—if ancient—roof above their heads.

The widowed Mrs. Wyndham had been persuaded to accept on the understanding both she and her unmarried daughter, Galatea, would educate Polly and make her fit for Society. Hal wanted Polly brought up in the strictest of regimes, for he planned to send her away to board at Miss Gates' Academy for Young Ladies in Selbury, in the far south of the county.

Polly would need to be tough, both inside and out, to cope with the stigma of having such notorious parents, the—*allegedly*—adulterous Lady Mary Ansford and her—*allegedly*—murderous husband.

How quick Society had been to condemn.

Hal picked up the most recent letter from Finchingfield and took it across to the lantern to re-examine its contents, but he was still distracted by bitterness. It seemed a man could lead a blameless, even laudable life, win the acclaim of his peers, and be the most admired nobleman in the West of England, but be deemed the very devil the moment something disastrous occurred in his personal life. Where was the sympathy, the understanding? Society had been so determined to blame him after Mary's death, he hadn't even bothered to refute the rumors. He'd simply told Society it could go hang and taken himself and Polly out of it.

He returned his attention to the letter. So, it was all arranged. The Wyndhams would be coming toward the end of May. The duke, along with Hal's steward Lynch, and his housekeeper, Mrs. Dunne, had attended to the details. Rather than allow his new family to spend any longer in that soul-destroying poorhouse than they needed to, Hal had provided money to set them up with accommodation in one of the better parts of Selbury, where they could hold their heads up high, rub shoulders with the *ton* if they cared to, and be comfortable in every way.

When the Wyndhams eventually arrived at Foxleaze, they must be in full health and looks and be the picture of respectability. What little pride Hal had left demanded it—and he also firmly believed Polly would be more likely to take notice of a pair of smart, upright-looking females.

But were they smart? Were they upright? He'd debated this question a long time and ultimately asked Finchingfield to not only inquire into their history but also appeal to his wife Lucy, for some idea of the character of the two ladies.

This letter contained the answers to both his questions. Sarah Wyndham was reported as being unremarkable in any way, apart from too proud to accept charity. Her daughter, Galatea, had been a friend of Lucy's for many years, since they'd attended Miss Gates' Academy together as girls.

This, in Hal's book, was an excellent reference, as it was the selfsame school where he meant to send his daughter. Miss Gates had a reputation for ruling her pupils with a rod of iron, the perfect way of giving Polly the backbone she was going to need when she became part of the world beyond the walls of Foxleaze Abbey.

Exactly what the Wyndhams would do with their time when Polly was sent off to school, he wasn't certain. But so long as it didn't impinge on him, and his activities, he didn't really care.

His eyes wandered once again to the final sentence in Finchingfield's letter. It was the only thing about the entire arrangement that perturbed him and made him wonder if he wasn't about to make the worst mistake of his life.

Miss Galatea Wyndham, or Tia for short, is well-educated, openhearted, graceful, joyful and, so my wife tells me, beautiful both inside and out. Polly will love her. You will both love her.

He chewed on his lip, folded the letter away, and stared unblinkingly at the gray walls of his self-imposed prison.

The last thing he wanted was to love anybody.

Ever again.

Chapter 2

On a damp, unseasonably cold afternoon in late May, Tia and her mama arrived at Foxleaze Abbey. Despite the forbidding aspect created by the gloomy weather, Tia was delighted by the modern honey-colored facade of the building and professed herself fascinated by the medley of uneven roof lines and turrets behind it, proclaiming its more ancient past.

So long as no ghostly nuns—or late baronesses—lurked in the crypts or corridors, she could be exceedingly happy in such a place. Compared to the poorhouse, it was heaven— there was so much space, so much architectural beauty, and such splendidly landscaped grounds.

If only Polly Pelham proved to be an amenable child, and her father not nearly so peculiar—or dangerous—as rumor suggested, Tia decided she could grow to love the place in no time.

A smartly dressed lady bobbed a curtsy as she and Mama entered the building. "Good day to you. I am Mrs. Dunne, Lord Ansford's housekeeper. Please follow me."

In no time at all, their luggage had been brought inside and taken upstairs. "May I offer you refreshment or a brief tour of the house?" Mrs. Dunne inquired.

Tia shot a hopeful look at her mama. "Oh, I should much prefer to see the house, for it seems the kind of place one might get lost in, so best start finding our way around immediately. Assuming you're fit to wait a short while longer for your tea, Mama?"

Hugely improved in both health and mind since their escape from the poorhouse, Mama nodded her agreement. "Is your master away at present?"

Was that a flash of awareness staining the housekeeper's cheeks? About what was she embarrassed?

"No, madam, he is not away."

"Has he not been told of our arrival?" Surely, he must have noticed their carriage.

"I regret his Lordship does not wish to be disturbed at present."

Tia exchanged a glance with Mama. How unutterably rude of him not to be here to welcome his guests. Not so much peculiar as ill-mannered. This did not bode well.

"Oh, how disappointing." She laughed lightly. "I hope he's not avoiding us deliberately."

The housekeeper said quickly, "No, indeed, miss. But his Lordship is always occupied. He does most of his work at home and goes out no more than he needs to. But that's not to say you may not make social calls of your own. There are riding horses available and both winter and summer carriages at your disposal, as well as a curricle if either of you ladies cares to drive."

Tia brightened. No, she didn't know how to drive a carriage, having been brought up in the busy port of Southampton where the roads were too clogged to be safe. But she'd love to learn. There must be many splendid sights hereabouts, and what a wonderful sense of freedom it must give to be able to drive oneself. She would take Polly out with her.

Would Lord Ansford have the patience to teach her to drive? Or even the inclination to do so? Lucy had tried to enlighten Tia as to Lord Ansford's character, but it seemed the more she heard about him, the less she knew.

That matter could be put aside for now. First, she must learn to find her way around the house. She could hardly expect her new pupil to respect her if she were constantly getting lost.

Despite the modern facade, much of the original abbey remained. There were some obvious Tudor period renovations, including the addition of wooden paneling and vast brick fireplaces. These had presumably been added after the Dissolution by the new lay owners, to make the place more like a home and less like an institution.

Tia shuddered. After the poorhouse, she never wanted to set foot inside an institution again.

As she followed her mama and the housekeeper through the maze of passageways, she discovered her new home was a real hotchpotch of different styles and intentions, testament to the wealth and taste—or lack thereof—of many generations of Pelhams.

As they ascended a sweeping staircase, a dark oak affair of the previous century, she paused in front of a multifaceted window of yellowed glass. This ancient insertion shone a sickly light onto the half landing and the menacing suit of armor set there as adornment. Through the glass Tia could make out the wavy shapes of trees and, realizing how high up she was, she impulsively opened the window to see what manner of view it afforded.

"Oh!" The sight that met her eyes was the very last thing she'd expected to see.

A half-naked man strode past the house.

She stood and stared, transfixed by his grace as he walked barefoot across the lawn, his dark gold hair hanging in damp tendrils down his back, only partially concealing the well-defined musculature of his torso. His sole item of clothing was a pair of soaked black breeches, clinging revealingly to his muscular thighs. He was wringing something out in his hands as he walked. His shirt, perhaps?

Well, who'd have imagined Lord Ansford employed a hermit? Tia knew some members of the aristocracy kept them, for the amusement of their friends. Oh, to have the money to waste on such foolishness. The hapless creatures were expected to live in caves or grottoes, often constructed in the previous century when the building of fanciful follies on country estates was highly popular.

Something hung about the hermit's neck and swung as he walked, but he was already too far away for her to identify it. A crucifix, perhaps? The man continued on in the direction of a stand of tall trees and melted from view when a sudden squall of rain cut across Tia's vision.

As she struggled to close the ancient catch of the window, she refused to be shocked by what she'd seen. Fascinating, though. Might the man be not only a hermit but a flagellant as well? But no—she'd seen no marks on his pale flesh. Maybe there was such a thing as a partial flagellant, someone who exposed themselves to the rain and the cold as a penance but didn't go so far as beating themselves with sticks. Perhaps the black garment he'd been holding was his horsehair shirt.

She hoped not. Concealing such a splendid body beneath a hair shirt would be like putting a frock coat on a Praxiteles—all that masculine magnificence hidden away . . .

As Tia hurried to catch up with her mama and the housekeeper, she wondered what young Polly thought about this hermit. Surely the sight of him was enough to terrify a child, and the idea of him lurking in some rocky cave within the grounds might deter her from venturing out alone.

She'd talk to Lord Ansford about it—when he finally made an appearance. Half-naked men wandering around the place did not create a comfortable environment for a gently bred young girl.

Nor—as the heat suffusing her own cheeks testified— did it create a comfortable environment for a woman of one-and-twenty.

Chapter 3

As the tour continued, it became increasingly apparent to Tia she was not to have as much freedom in her new home as she'd hoped. Various places were out of bounds, including the croquet lawn at the front of the house. The entire east wing of the building was utterly forbidden, since that was where Lord Ansford held sway, and he didn't want to be disturbed. There was mention too of the folly, within the grounds and in use, therefore also forbidden.

In use? Surely the whole point of a folly was that it had no use, apart from being a blatant show of wealth and adding interest to the gardens. Tia would have liked to question the housekeeper about the hermit she'd seen but dared not. Letting herself think about the semi-naked man had a powerful impact on her composure and would definitely put her to the blush.

The end of the tour brought them to the west wing of the house where she and Mama had been allocated their own bedchambers with attached dressing rooms, and a private sitting room to share between them.

"Miss Pelham sleeps in the nursery further along, where she's looked after by Nurse," Mrs. Dunne stated. "Now, shall I have tea sent up to your sitting—ah, here's Nurse herself. Miss Oates, meet Mrs. Wyndham and Miss Wyndham."

Miss Oates, who'd just issued from one of the nearby rooms, bustled forward to make her curtsy. She appeared kindly enough, but there was a wariness about her Tia found odd.

As Miss Oates and the housekeeper headed toward the stairs, Tia and her mama investigated their new living arrangements. Yet she couldn't help but think on the tragedy this household had suffered a little less than three years ago. Perhaps there was a reason for its inhabitants to seem somewhat . . . haunted.

Lucy had informed them of the horrid event in a letter she'd sent to confirm the final arrangements for their removal to Foxleaze. Lucy's husband the duke had shared what he'd come to know about Lord Ansford through the man's political successes and his vociferous campaign to hasten the abolition of slavery in every land subject to the British Crown.

A cause deemed worthy by many, but one taking up so much of the baron's time, he was reputed to have neglected his wife, a bright young thing with whom he was known to have been deeply, if unfashionably, in love.

What followed, Lucy declared to be mere rumor, and she'd begged Tia to tear up and burn the letter after she'd read it, lest Lord Ansford should ever chance upon it.

Tia wandered across to the small sitting room's stone-set window and gazed down onto the croquet lawn and the carriage drive below. She opened the window, despite the steady drizzle of rain. The habit of opening virtually every window she came upon had developed after her grim sojourn in Selbury Poorhouse, where she'd never been able to look out of one because they were too high up.

Briefly, Tia pondered Lucy's last letter. Ansford's neglected wife supposedly took lovers while her husband was up in Town. She had remained at Foxleaze for Polly's sake, as she loved to play with the child.

If the late baroness's affaires had been conducted in London, there would doubtless be more than mere gossip about with whom, how often, and when she'd had them. But in the country, it was possible to evade such eagle eyes and wagging tongues—if one was careful about it.

What had happened at the end of the baroness's short life was unclear. Officially, she had fallen from one of the towers. Asking further was indelicate, to say the least. Perhaps Lord Ansford, when Tia got to know him better, might give her the story himself.

But the most important fact remained, Lucy's husband and every one of their acquaintances completely rejected the gossip laying the cause of Lady Ansford's fall at her husband's door.

"Tia, come away from the window, or you'll catch a chill."

"Sorry, Mama. I'll shut it."

But Tia wasn't ready to sit down yet. She'd been cooped up in a coach for two hours, bursting with curiosity as to what her new home—and her new relations—would be like, and she was itching to explore further. "I'm going to stroll to the end of the corridor and back while we wait for tea to be brought up. I haven't stretched my legs enough."

At her mother's nod, she left the room, then hesitated. There were voices coming from the chamber she'd been told was the nursery.

Her heart flipped. One of the voices was high and childish. Polly, no doubt. The other was deep and strange. Was Lord Ansford himself in the very next room, talking to his daughter? Would it be dreadfully rude of her to poke her head in and see, and introduce herself to him?

Curiosity won out. The nurse had left the door ajar, so Tia peered through the crack into the room beyond and was astonished to see only one occupant, a small girl with tow-colored hair and dark eyes, sitting straight-backed in a wicker chair and dandling a doll on her lap.

Tia smiled. A child who played with dolls was normal

enough, even if said doll was dressed in trousers and had an eerily deep voice.

"Now Polly," the male doll was made to say, "you must eat up all your porridge, even if it reminds you of sick. If you are a very good girl, I might let you have a kitten, but you must keep it out from under my feet, d'ye hear? Yes, I will come and see you more often, I promise. It's only that I'm so busy all the time."

Polly replied, in her own voice, "You always say that, Papa, and you hardly ever come. You know I've no mama anymore, so you should come and see me twice as much, to make up for it."

"You are such a bad child," Polly's pretend father retorted. "You always ask for far too much."

Perhaps I'm not going to like Lord Ansford after all.

Even so, Tia plastered on her most cheerful expression and marched into the room.

Polly immediately stowed the doll beneath a cushion and got to her feet. She stared briefly before looking at the floor, then executed an awkward curtsy.

"I am Miss Wyndham. Your new—" Tia paused. Goodness, what was she? A companion, a teacher, a distant cousin? "I'm your new governess," she continued, thinking the title would serve for now, although she hoped she might one day be accorded the title of friend.

The girl gave no answer but remained standing with her back ramrod straight, studying her shoes.

"I assume you are Miss Mary Pelham." Tia tried to keep her tone light, encouraging. "Although I hope I may call you Polly."

Polly merely shrugged.

Goodness, in Miss Gates' Academy, anyone who made such a rude, dismissive gesture would be put on bread and water for a week. Even the poorhouse children had such behavior beaten out of them—and none of them would ever be in the same social circles Polly Pelham was likely to frequent.

Was the child truly sullen, or simply shy?

An image of her deceased sister Phoebe's face swam before Tia's eyes. Though Phoebe had been gone many years, her loss continued to cut Tia like a knife. And made her castigate herself about things she should have said to her sibling while Phoebe was alive, the small acts of kindness she could have performed.

It stiffened her resolve not to be put off by Polly's manner. The child needed encouragement, understanding, and love. Tia would do her best to provide all three.

"I can see I've caught you at a bad moment. We will no doubt meet later." She backed out of the room.

Rather than be dispirited by this inauspicious beginning, Tia vowed to talk to the nurse as well as the girl's father and find out how best to deal with a child who preferred talking to toys than to real people.

Closing the door softly on her new charge, Tia proceeded to the end of the passageway where a large crown glass window afforded a view across what must surely be the original abbey cloisters.

This window, too, she opened, to suck in a bracing breath of air and dispel the unease that had stolen upon her during her eavesdropping on Polly and their subsequent meeting.

Her hand flew to her throat.

He was there, the hermit, right below the window, staring up at her. She swallowed hard. What did one do with a hermit? Nod, wave, say, "Good afternoon?" Completely at a loss, she simply gazed at the fearsome creature, with his lank, dark gold locks and his black slashes of eyebrows. Fortunately, he had now donned his shirt, saving her blushes, but it was damp enough to cling to his frame.

She'd expected a hermit's body to be all skin and bone, but this man was sinewy and slim, although the clinging black shirt revealed the well-developed muscles of someone who exercised religiously.

Tia was struck forcibly by an image she recalled from Malory's *Le Morte D'Arthur*, that of Sir Lancelot run mad and lost in the wilderness, unkempt, long-haired; wild-eyed.

She suppressed a shiver. Yes, Lord Ansford's hermit was definitely frightful, not only to children but to adults as well.

She'd made up her mind to show her disapproval of him by shutting the window with no sign of acknowledgement, when he turned his back on her and stalked off into the cloisters.

What odd behavior.

If it weren't for the relative normality of Mrs. Dunne, Tia might imagine she'd wandered into a chapter of Walpole's *The Castle of Otranto*.

"Ah, Miss Wyndham, your tea has arrived." The voice spoke so close to her ear, it made her jump. Tia turned, to find Mrs. Dunne right by her elbow, carrying an ancient cow-shaped creamer.

Yet another thing to unnerve her today—servants who crept up on one in complete silence.

She was about to thank the housekeeper when Mrs. Dunne added, "I see you have been making the acquaintance of Lord Ansford."

Tia froze. That disheveled, manner-less creature was Lord Ansford? Her distant cousin, her new employer, her benefactor, and the owner of Foxleaze?

If that were truly so, it was possible the stories of him as a madman who'd murdered his wife in a jealous rage . . .

Might not be rumors after all.

Chapter 4

The Wyndhams had only been in residence a day and a night, and already Hal's old anxieties were flooding back. He'd thought his backbreaking labors, his strict physical regime, and the amount of time he devoted to honoring his dead wife's memory would have appeased her spirit.

Yet every time he ventured to please or reward himself, her ghost would rise up to chastise him.

The memory of her last cruel words to him resurfaced and repeated themselves like a chant in his head. *You're worthless. You're a pathetic husband, a useless father, an eminently forgettable lover. I despise you.*

Of course, Mary hadn't meant those words, had she? She'd been ill, not herself, and he must never forget the fact. But he feared there was a kernel of truth in every word she spoke.

Except for the lover part. That aspect of their marriage had given great pleasure to them both, but Mary's appetites, it seemed, could not be satiated by a husband who devoted so much of his time to his work.

And Polly looked a good deal like her mother.

As Hal mounted the stairs to the top of the folly, he reassured himself—yet again—that his daughter would not take after Mary in character. His wife had been gay but selfish, beautiful yet vain, as witty as she was incisive. He would do whatever was needed to make sure Polly never took after her mother. A few years at Miss Gates' Academy would turn her into a truly respectable and proper young lady. When it came time to find a husband for her, she would be so poised, so perfect, the vicissitudes of her parents and dark family history would be completely forgotten.

When he reached the roof, he came out into sunshine. As he always did, he walked right up to the battlements and directed his gaze downward, to test himself. One day he would be able to view the steep drop with equanimity. Not that anyone was ever likely to throw themselves to their death from the top of the folly again . . .

Unless, perhaps, that someone was himself, when the black despair overwhelmed him.

An unexpected movement caught him up short. Three people were strolling across the lawns in the direction of the sheep pasture.

The smallest of them was clearly Polly. He always experienced a pang upon seeing her. Whether it was guilt, pain, or dislike, he had yet to fathom. Generally, he found it easier not to think about her much at all. One of the women kept falling behind due to her slower pace. Mrs. Sarah Wyndham, no doubt. She appeared refined and well-dressed, and he congratulated himself on having made his distant relatives a generous allowance for clothing. They had good taste in apparel.

The other woman, who walked close to Polly, was quick and determined in her walk. Good. A brisk character was exactly the kind to which Polly would respond.

If only the Wyndham girl didn't walk quite so close to her. They even brushed elbows a few times, as the sway of their bodies crossing the rougher ground of the pasture brought them together. It made the trio resemble a loving family far too much.

And a loving family was something he could not condone. A loving family was something of which he couldn't be a part.

Ever.

With his heart dead inside him, discipline was all that remained, all that kept him going.

As he continued to watch, Miss Wyndham paused, bent, and examined something by her feet.

In response to her invitation, Polly bent down as well.

Something was plucked from the ground, and as Polly and her new tutor stood up straight again, the Wyndham chit placed it in his daughter's hair, before standing back to appraise her.

Hal clenched his jaw. He hadn't invited the Wyndhams into his home to have them indulge in such foolishness as putting flowers in a young girl's hair. Polly was not a toy with which to be played. Yes, he knew the Wyndhams had lost a daughter in the past, and he was sorry for it, but that gave them no excuse to be soft on Polly.

In fact, this sort of familiar behavior was the exact opposite of what he wanted for her. He would have a word with Miss Wyndham.

A cold sweat broke out on his brow, making him scrub irritably at his forehead. Deuce take it, why was he anxious again? Perhaps because he hadn't had a normal conversation with anyone since Mary's death. Could he even recall how to go about it? It would mean meeting his new dependents face-to-face.

Yes, he had already seen Miss Wyndham, but she'd nothing to say to him, which didn't help the situation at all. A note would have to do. He'd write it now and give it to one of the servants to deliver.

Miss Galatea Wyndham needed to be taken to task immediately, before she completely scuppered his plans.

Chapter 5

"Infuriating man!"

Tia stalked from one side of the breakfast room to the other, crumpling the piece of paper in her hands. It was as much as she could do not to tear it into myriad pieces and individually set fire to them from the plate warmer on the sideboard. Except such action might cause a conflagration, completely ruining breakfast—and burning down their new home when they'd been in it a mere three days.

Not the wisest of actions.

"Calm down, my dear. Is it so very terrible Lord Ansford should write to you thus?"

"It's inexpressibly rude, Mama, that's what it is." Tia flopped into a chair and poked angrily at the slice of ham on her plate. "He hasn't even introduced himself to us yet, but he's already ordering us about like servants."

"Well, in a way we are."

"But we're also family, despite being only distantly related."

"Very distantly," Mama echoed.

"So, he should accord us a bit more respect. I mean, me in particular, as this missive doesn't mention you. Clearly, I am the only one at fault."

Her mother heaved a great sigh. "I fully understand you find his tone peremptory—"

"To say the least."

"But we mustn't forget he may not be in his right mind."

"After three years? Surely anyone recovers from the loss

of a spouse in three years—oh, please forgive me. That was insensitive."

Mama dabbed at her eyes with a napkin. When she raised her head, her mouth was set in a determined line.

"We promised each other not to ruin our lives with grief. Being in the poorhouse has stiffened my resolve not to repine. I will never forget your papa, and nor must you, but you can see what lengthy grieving can do to a person. It is most unhealthy."

"I will never forget Papa, nor little Phoebe. I treasure their memories, but as you say, it's unwise to submerge oneself in misery. It seems to have unhinged Lord Ansford entirely."

Mama took a sip of her Darjeeling. "Therefore, we must be patient with him. And never forget he is our benefactor. Do you really want to hazard our futures on a matter of principle?"

Tia uncrumpled the note and smoothed it out beside her breakfast plate, steeling herself to read it one more time so she could decide what action to take.

Miss Wyndham, the note said, *I trust you will not pamper Miss Polly with any approaches of friendship. I thought I had made myself clear when I explained she must be educated under the strictest of regimens. A sociable meander about the grounds with yourself and Mrs. Wyndham does not come under the aegis of "education." It is merely a waste of time. Should Polly require exercise, she can take it with Nurse.*

The note was signed with an aristocratic scrawl.

"I don't intend to change my attitude toward Polly." Tia struggled to keep the defiance from her voice. "I stand by my belief she needs to be won over gradually, with kindness and understanding. And she deserves to have some enjoyment, after what she's been through. After what her father is still putting her through."

At her mother's wry expression, Tia added, "I promise to be careful not to anger or upset Lord Ansford. I'm certain he will understand when I explain my proposed methods to him. I'll be subtle and reasonable. I don't want you worrying he might fly into a rage and turn us out."

"Fortunately, that isn't something he can easily do. His duty to us is all bound up in law, as his man of business explained before we arrived. Ansford has even made us beneficiaries in his will, though I cannot understand why so young a man considered he needed to make one."

"He evidently does not wish to allow room for error. I think he likes to be in control. Of everything. And I wouldn't call him young," Tia mused. "Why, he seemed at least forty to me."

"Goodness, no! I'm certain he's barely reached thirty. Such a shame so promising a political career should be cut short by tragedy."

Tia signaled to the waiting footman, who withdrew her chair as she stood. Thanking him with a nod, she walked across to the mullioned window. Quaint though these historical items of architecture were, the leaded panes did not give a good view of the gardens beyond, adding to her sense of being shut in.

The catch gave with a metallic clang, but she paused a moment before pushing the window open. What if he were outside, glaring back at her with those dark, storm-filled eyes and that heavy, disapproving frown?

This is nonsense.

She had no reason to fear the man, none at all. He would hardly have opened his home to them if he meant them any harm.

Would he?

She pulled the window to and spun on her heel, catching a resigned expression on her mother's face. She ignored it.

"I'm going right now in search of him." *Before my courage fails me.*

"But you don't know where he is," Mama pointed out.

"Well, I know where he won't be. With Polly. She told me yesterday she barely sees him from one week to the next. I shall boldly penetrate the forbidden east wing, and if I don't find him there, he's probably in that horrid folly tower Mrs. Dunne told us to stay away from."

"Not without good reason, I'm sure." Mama raised an eyebrow in warning.

"Polly's starting to speak up a bit more now, and I need her to trust me. If I bring out the birch switch and act the martinet, she'll only retreat into herself again. I'm sorry, but for Polly's sake I must do this."

It was for her own sake as well, though she cared not to admit it. It wasn't pleasant, being ignored.

"I promise not to be cross," she reassured her mother. "By the time I've tracked down the lion to his lair, the exercise will have made me more equable."

Leaving Mama to the excitements of the *North Wiltshire Gazette*, Tia left the breakfast room and headed for the main hallway. Once there, instead of turning left toward their wing of the house, she spun to the right and stood for a moment facing down the door into the east wing. With its thick oak panels and iron studs, it resembled the gate of a fortress. For a moment she feared it might be locked and barred to her, and she'd have to find some other way in.

But when she applied her hand to the ring, it turned easily. A lift of the latch, one foot forward, and she was in Terra Incognita.

Not only unknown but also forbidden.

Chapter 6

As Tia went through the doorway, a breath of cold air made her shiver. She had emerged into the abbey's medieval cloister, with the rose garden at its center. As she gazed around, empty doorways gaped with black maws from the walkways, and when she glanced up, it was to find herself being leered at by roof bosses carved into grotesque creatures.

She repressed a shudder. What would she discover if she explored this place? The skeletons of innumerable murdered wives and relations? An antiquated torture chamber? Her sense of unease was not improved by the fact the weather had now broken. Dark clouds scudded across the sky, casting fistfuls of rain against the windows, with only a crash of thunder or a blast of lightning lacking to complete the melodramatic effect.

Tia hurried on until she came to a stretch of cloister apparently more inhabited than the other parts. At the foot of a stone stairway stood a shoe rack, a boot remover, and a foot-scraper, set beneath a line of pegs containing a range of caped coats, cloaks, and gentleman's hats.

So, Lord Ansford was human after all. Here was the paraphernalia of everyday existence, items belonging to a flesh and blood man. Not a wife-killing fiend or lunatic flagellant, but a real being who got his boots muddy and enjoyed protection from the cold.

This was the staircase she must try, in hopes of finally meeting the master of Foxleaze face to face. The steps led up to a corridor lined with bookcases. Tia gasped as she scanned the titles—histories, geographies, art engravings, travels, Chapman's *Homer*, Dryden's translation of *Virgil*, Caesar's *The Gallic Wars*.

When all the Wyndham's books had to be sold, she'd been distraught. How ungenerous of the baron to forbid them this treasure house of knowledge. But perhaps he didn't know of her deprivation and would perfectly understand if she asked for access to his library.

Remembering the prime reason for her foray, Tia dragged herself away and continued her exploration. A bit farther along the corridor, she came upon a gentleman's study, complete with walnut-topped desk, studded leather chair, and various writing implements. The room boasted a magnificent marble fireplace, currently sporting a display of lilac blooms, lavender, and white roses.

The guilt-ridden, wife-murdering, relative-hating Lord Ansford receded into the background of her imagination and an accomplished scholar with excellent taste took his place.

Glancing about in pleasant surprise, Tia noticed a large portrait hanging above the fireplace. A closer examination revealed the skill of its painter. He—or she—had captured the skin tones of the female subject perfectly and had picked out where the light reflected in the woman's gray eyes and gleamed in her guinea-gold locks. The artist's brush had recorded every fold of the gown and the individual curls of the sitter's hair where they caressed her face.

This was Polly's mother.

There was no doubting the similarity. The late baroness was portrayed as a breathtaking, golden beauty. With her own dark curls and brown eyes, Tia considered herself no more than a common country wench in the presence of so much ethereal pallor.

So absorbed was she in contemplation of the former Lady Ansford, she didn't hear the measured tread behind her, nor the sharp intake of breath signaling the newcomer's arrival.

A harsh voice behind her rasped, "This room is private."

Tia jumped in shock, spun around, and found herself face to face with the owner of Foxleaze Abbey.

Fortunately—or otherwise—the man was fully dressed. Had he not been, it would have been a struggle to keep her eyes from straying admiringly across the superb musculature of his torso. Now it was hidden beneath somber black clothing, which accentuated the paleness of his skin and echoed the dark circles around his eyes. Did he never raise his face to the sun? Did he never sleep?

If any gentleman had set out to make himself appear frightful, Lord Ansford was that gentleman.

He continued to glare at her, his words a challenge hanging in the air between them like a duelist's glove.

She met his regard directly, and suddenly the masculine beauty hidden behind the unkempt hair and straggling beard was revealed to her. Long, dark, feathered lashes. High, aristocratic cheekbones. Combined with the black slashes of his eyebrows, his features looked as if they'd been applied by the hand of a master.

Her eyes snagged on his firm mouth—it had a fascinating tilt at each corner, though his lips were unsmiling. He boasted a straight nose and determined, square jaw, speckled with dark stubble.

Here was a man with enough excellent physical attributes to make every woman in the land fall at his feet—but he didn't give a damn.

Moistening lips gone suddenly dry, Tia started forward, one hand outstretched in greeting. "Lord Ansford, we meet at last. I am Galatea Wyndham. Delighted to make your acquaintance."

"I know who you are." As his hands remained clasped behind his back, she dropped her own in confusion and fiddled with a fold of her skirts. How unforgivably rude! But she mustn't rise to the bait and forget her purpose in coming here.

Polly. It was all about Polly.

"You should not be here," Ansford continued in the same colorless tone. "You must leave at once."

Not only rude but hurtful. How did one make any headway with such a creature?

By setting a good example and by not sinking to his level.

"Forgive me, my lord. I didn't mean to intrude upon your privacy. I thought the place empty and was just admiring the splendid portrait above the fireplace."

Ansford continued to observe her in a disinterested fashion, which, paradoxically, unnerved her more than outright animosity would have done. Should she swallow her pride and go?

He was waiting for her to do exactly that. She sensed stubbornness behind the facade of indifference, willpower that would eventually drive her from the room with nary a word spoken.

Direct conflict with the man who held the Wyndhams' fate in his hands? Not a good plan. She would have to see if she could draw him out somehow, make her presence less odious to him.

Glancing at the portrait above the fireplace, she began conversationally, "Who's the artist? They're a true master of their craft."

"You'd recognize a master's hand, would you?"

She shot him a sharp look, but his face remained impassive.

"I'm educated well enough to know about art, my lord. You wouldn't have employed me to teach Polly if you thought otherwise. I used to visit all the exhibitions—"

He waved her into silence. "I don't mean to indulge in conversation, Miss Wyndham. I'm waiting for you to leave."

What abominable rudeness! Fissures started to appear in her resolve.

"Of course, I'll quit your study if I'm disturbing you. But I'd like to be allowed to make use of your library. Some of the books will complement Polly's studies."

"No."

The fissures became chasms.

"I promise I'll do nothing to disturb you." She strove to keep the terseness from her voice.

"I said no."

Tia chewed on her lip. Handsome as a statue of a Greek god. With a heart as hard as marble. But she wasn't prepared to give up. Yet.

"I can always send a servant for a book," she offered. "You must allow your staff up here."

One dark brow lifted. It was the first sign he'd given of any real emotion.

"You can hardly expect my servants to recognize a name like 'Aeschylus' when they see it written down, or 'Euripides.' Fetch you a book they will," he informed her, "but it won't be the one you sent for."

Two sentences from the implacable Lord Ansford? This could almost be considered progress.

"If I wrote the title down for them, clearly and carefully," she persisted, "they would be able to match it up with the appropriate book."

The other eyebrow joined its fellow. "Do you have any idea how long it would take a servant to match up your writing to the book title? No, I want as little disturbance as possible. I cannot have footmen with lighted lamps poring for hours through my library. It is unthinkable."

It might be unthinkable now, but she would find a way.

Let's see who of the two of us is the most immovable.

She bowed her head, a polite but insincere acknowledgment of his victory. "Good morning, my lord. Perhaps we may see you at dinner?"

She was hoping no such thing, for his presence would cast a pall of gloom across the table and make every dish taste like ashes.

He made no reply as she eased past him and made for the door. His indifference infuriated her more than his anger might have done.

She didn't like failing to make an impression, she didn't like feeling unwanted, and more than anything she hated not being accorded the common courtesies. Her benefactor was a damnable fellow, and she had no desire to set eyes on him ever again, or listen to his colorless voice, or see his emotionless face.

Yet Tia couldn't help but glance over her shoulder to see if her defiance had wrought any change in the man's demeanor, elicited any expression he didn't want her to see.

No. He'd simply turned his back on the door and was staring up at the portrait, as impervious to Tia as he was to the rest of the world. And if she didn't like being ignored, well, it was her cross to bear.

But the lure of that library—

For her own sake, as much as for Polly's, she would have to find some way around Lord Ansford's nonsensical rules. Otherwise, her future life at Foxleaze Abbey was going to be frustrating in the extreme.

Chapter 7

Hal picked up a chisel and applied it to the stone, then struck hard with his mason's hammer. A chip flew off and grazed his cheek, but he relished the pain.

Pain proved he was alive. Pain proved he was still paying Mary back for all the harm he had done to her.

The sound of steel on stone echoed about the chamber, its stridency at odds with the dark, silent chill of the folly tower. Hal's mouth quirked—here he was, challenging the ghosts again, spirits whose inimical eyes had, it seemed, watched him all his life.

He'd believed himself accursed from the age of seven. That was the year his pony tossed him into a dry ditch and put him in bed for a month, thus terminating all his pleasures for what seemed like a lot longer. Seven was also the age he began to believe in ghostly nuns, evil witches, headless horsemen, and spirit animals, any number of which could be imagined haunting the echoing passageways of Foxleaze Abbey.

Hal brushed at the grit adhering to his chest. Soon he would resemble a phantom himself, covered in white dust, with only his eyes visible through the crust, wild and staring. How fortunate it was to have the river running through the Foxleaze estate. A way not only of mortifying the flesh but of cleansing himself.

On the whole, he had grown out of those childhood fears. Or perhaps the ghosts had ceased to torment him because he'd attempted to live an exemplary life. He'd spoken out against slavery, voiced his opinion about the Corn Laws, and criticized the government for using agitators to infiltrate those amongst the lower classes who were campaigning for reform. Having won their trust, the agitators represented them all as Jacobins and a threat to national security.

Campaigning for the downtrodden was all well and good while he was the heir to Foxleaze, but his responsibilities increased monumentally when he came into the title. This led to more misunderstandings with his wife, primarily because he had no time to ensure any disputes between them were amicably settled.

Hal winced as he recalled the years immediately preceding Mary's death. He hated himself for growing dourer, quicker to anger. Presents and promises were given in lieu of his attention, but it sometimes struck him he and his wife were leading such different lives, they might as well not be married at all. And they'd seemed to argue all the time.

As he lined up the chisel for another blow, Hal recalled how he'd deliberately stay up late poring over his papers so he could avoid deciding whether or not to go to her bed. Inevitably he ran the risk of censure either way.

Gradually rumors began to circulate Mary had taken a lover.

Possibly more than one.

At first, Hal thought it was simply a case of political rivals—men with no moral scruples whatsoever—trying to disquiet him and send him running back to the country.

And go back he had, eventually. Only to find his wife in a precarious state of both mind and health. She'd obstinately refused to talk to him about it or give him the name of the physician she was seeing. When he found the small bottles of mercury in her jewelry box, the cruel truth had hit him with the force of a charging bull.

Syphilis.

He struck another blow at the marble, the base this time, so he could vent his rage without damaging his more delicate work. There must have been something he could have done to prevent her developing this awful malady.

If he hadn't left her so much on her own . . .

Then had come the fateful day when he'd been at the top of the folly, attempting a sketch of the Mary he remembered, young, fresh, and beautiful. She'd come out to speak to him—for what reason, he never discovered—and he watched her halting progress across the lawns, sorrowing at how thin and awkward she was compared with that lively diamond of the *ton* she'd been when he first met her.

In retrospect, he should have gone down to see what she wanted. But anger had gripped him, anger that she'd thrown away everything they'd ever shared together and made herself sick into the bargain, and anger at himself for letting it happen.

It took her a long time to reach the top of the folly, and by the time she'd emerged onto the roof, her face was pale and oily with perspiration, her chest heaving raggedly from her exertions.

Her mouth had formed a pinched, disapproving line when she saw him watching her. "I disgust you now, don't I?"

"Not at all. I'm sad for you. I want you to be well again. Why don't you go back to bed?"

This had been a bone of contention between them ever since he'd discovered how ill she was. It was his belief she should be pampered, remaining in bed, attended by the best physicians in the land, with himself and Polly paying regular visits to stop her from getting bored.

She had stubbornly refused to accept his advice, going about her household tasks with an obsessive ardor he'd never seen in her before.

Mary had glared back at him, her red-rimmed eyes dark with malice. "I have no intention of wasting the short time I have left simply lazing in bed."

She'd hobbled toward him. Her legs were tightly bandaged to contain the incipient ulcers, making it harder for her to walk. She often complained the bandages were so tight, her feet went numb.

He'd put down his sketchbook and resigned himself to a tirade. He could read in her face that he had, yet again, unwittingly done something heinous. But her gaze fell on his sketchbook, and before he could stop her, she lurched forward and grabbed it.

"What have you been drawing? Oh!"

Too much the gentleman to snatch the book back, it would have been childish of him to fight her for it. And what, after all, did he have to hide? His artistic skill was good, and he'd made dozens of sketches and paintings of his wife in the early days of their marriage.

She turned her back on him and examined the drawing on which he'd been working. Then, glancing over her shoulder, she gave him a look which froze him to the marrow and began systematically tearing the sketch to pieces, dropping the scraps of paper between the crenellations of the folly, where they wafted down like feathers on the breeze.

"Mary, no!"

In response, she turned to him, eyes blazing. She spoke slowly, malevolently. "Henry Pelham. I. Hate. You."

What happened next would return to him in nightmares, relentlessly torturing him. Even when he was awake, he continually relived those moments, trying to determine if she had fallen deliberately or by accident.

The first physician who had seen her after Hal, sick to his core, had her broken, lifeless body conveyed back to the house, had proclaimed the fall an accident. The baroness's illness interfered with her balance, and the cures she took sometimes did more harm than good. It would have needed no more than a spell of dizziness or fainting when she was so close to the edge, to unbalance and tip her over.

Despite what Hal truly believed—that she had thrown herself from the tower to spite him as well as to end a life already doomed—he'd accepted the doctor's verdict.

As, luckily, did the rest of the world.

Bodies of suicide victims were not welcome in hallowed soil, and the chapel at Foxleaze Abbey was consecrated. For Mary's remains to be allowed to rest in the place she had called home, and where she'd borne and brought up her child, her death had to be put down to a tragic misadventure.

He blinked away the memories.

Mary had the power to wound him, even from the grave. She had ruined his life, had killed the man he once was and destroyed any hope of ever becoming the man he'd wanted to be.

His thoughts strayed unbidden to his recent encounter with Miss Wyndham. In some ways she was quite the opposite of Mary but in other ways, too similar for comfort. Galatea Wyndham had shaken him, though he'd refused to show it. He wasn't used to being disputed with in his own home— Mary was the last person who'd ever dared do such a thing. And that was where the similarity lay. Both women were a mixture of feminine wiles and downright stubbornness.

But if Miss Galatea Wyndham hoped to win him 'round with her dancing brown eyes and cheerful aspect, she had better think again.

Chapter 8

A full two weeks had passed since Tia's unpromising encounter with the reclusive Lord Ansford in his study, and neither she nor Mama had had more than a glimpse of him since.

He'd occasionally been seen striding across the lawns in the direction of his folly tower, not that she'd deliberately been trying to get a glimpse of him. Perhaps in view of the fact he now had two gentlewomen in the house, he no longer walked about shirtless which might—or might not—indicate some improvement in his character.

Seated in their snug sitting room, Tia and her mother shared a light supper. A summer shower had recently passed by, and the croquet lawn outside the window sparkled with fresh raindrops. The exotic rhododendrons lining the drive stood proudly in their freshly washed foliage, and fingers of sunlight picked out occasional droplets of water, filling them with a fiery gold.

It was a tranquil scene, entirely at odds with the one she had confronted earlier the same morning.

Tia cleared her throat. "I came upon his lordship's folly this morning." It was a hard admission to make—she'd breached The Rules and Mama would not approve.

"Did you, dear? I hope you were discreet."

"Oh, but I bumped into Lynch, who told me Lord Ansford had an appointment in town, so I knew the coast was clear."

Mama raised her eyebrows. "So, you didn't exactly 'come upon it,' did you?"

Ignoring the taunt, Tia went on, "It's in a clearing in the trees, but it must be visible from some of the windows in the east wing. There's a huge mound of granite boulders glued together with mortar containing a good deal of dark ash, presumably to match the color of the stone."

"It appears you made a close inspection of it." Mama helped herself to another slice of almond tart and regarded Tia thoughtfully.

"It's quite horrid," Tia persisted. "As I looked up at the tower, it was as if someone had walked on my grave. The sun went in, and I had this awful presentiment of doom, as though I were being watched by someone, or something, with evil intent."

"This place is melancholy when there's no sunlight to cheer it. But I'm sure there's nothing evil here. Lord Ansford would never allow it."

Unless he's a part of it, of course.

Tia had sensed the empty window embrasures as inimical eyes, watching her as she walked back to the abbey. An unwelcome crop of imaginings had crowded her mind at that moment. Could the folly tower be the spot where the late baroness had fallen to her doom? Did it hide a maze of tunnels or a secret room where Hellfire Clubbers held their abominably sinful, godless rituals?

She shook the ideas away. Mama would chide her for being fanciful if she said anything more. But now she'd seen the place, the folly lurked at the back of her mind, a mystery to be solved, an obstacle to overcome.

As was its owner.

Time to change the subject. "Polly and I are getting along quite comfortably now. I'm giving her work to stretch but not overwhelm her, as well as tasks so simple she has the instant satisfaction of achieving full marks. This will, I hope, increase her confidence. Why, we even managed some conversation yesterday. You know how fond I am of sketching birds? Well, there was a pair of long-tailed titmice in the orchard this morning. I identified them for her and commented on their pink and black and white plumage. She began asking me questions about them and why I liked birds and how was it possible to draw them when they would never stop moving? I won't say we became fast friends as a result of that exchange, but I consider it progress."

"You'd think Ansford would have been to the schoolroom by now, to ensure you are following his dictates."

"Ah, but that would mean having to converse with me, an activity he utterly detests. However, for Polly's sake, I have a plan to bring him forth. I'll take books from his library he's sure to consider most unsuitable for a young girl's education and leave obvious gaps, so he'll realize what's gone. He's sure to come stomping into the schoolroom, ready for a battle."

Her mother put down her pastry fork with a clatter. "I sincerely hope you won't fight in front of Polly. Tell me, do you think it wise to antagonize him when we are his dependents?"

"Trust me, Mama. Underneath the grim exterior, I believe Lord Ansford has a heart, and although it may be an awkward path to reach it, I'm prepared to try, for it will make him a better man."

"You mean to reach his heart?"

The shock in Mama's tone made Tia blush furiously. "You misunderstand me. I don't wish to win his heart, merely to set it beating again, to arouse the sort of paternal affection he ought to have for his child. Once he loves her as he should, he'll realize he mustn't send her away to Miss Gates's Academy. Polly divulged to me the other day she'd already been taken on an inspection visit of the place. She made no complaint, for Polly seldom shows her emotions, but I could tell she was terrified."

"Oh no, please say you're not going to make him one of your projects. You remember what happened last time. Poor Mr. Roach—he went around aping the Romantic poets for weeks after your interference, and let his hair grow so long all the young ladies looked at him askance."

Tia knew a pang of distress at this reminder of the Wyndhams' halcyon days. She was fifteen when she tried to 'improve' young Ralph Roach. Papa was alive, the wine import business flourished, and the family owned three ships, with additional ones on charter.

But in the 'Year Without a Summer' the vintages had been poor, the weather worse, the charters were let go, and two years later, in October 1818, a cruel gale had dashed her father and the 'Sarah Gay' onto rocks off the Cornish coast.

And afterward had come their removal to that hideous institution, the poorhouse, where husbands were separated from wives, where children were sundered from their parents—

"Don't be so downcast—I'm only teasing you. Mr. Roach is surely quite recovered—he must have reached his majority by now and will be well set up indeed and attractive to all the matchmaking mamas."

Tia forced herself to look amused, but her thoughts were no longer on Mr. Roach. Lord Ansford must see that sending Polly away would be wrong. She'd have to appeal to his finer feelings, if he had any. Surely, all the kindnesses bestowed on the Wyndhams could not have come from a man with no heart?

Unless they had his steward, Josiah Lynch, to thank for it all. She could well imagine Lord Ansford saying to him, "See to it, will you?" and taking no further interest.

Why the devil should she not try to reform the baron? He was desperately in need of it. He was only flesh and blood after all and must have some weakness she could exploit. If she could determine what his Achilles heel was, she'd soon have him behaving like a loving father toward Polly, hugely benefitting the child.

And it would make her own existence a good deal less uncomfortable.

Chapter 9

Hal kicked the marble dust off his shoes, sending a small shower of dark mortar to the floor. He really should clean this room, but somehow it never seemed important enough. The stairs leading up to the folly's door were gritty too, from weathering, but as his were the only feet ever to tread that way, he'd never seen fit to sweep them.

As he picked up his chisel once more, a sound from outside made him miss his mark. Cursing softly, he glared across at the embrasure, widened in this room to admit more light.

Where usually the only sound was the sighing of the wind in the trees or the shouts of rooks and clatter of pigeon wings, he could hear voices.

He turned again to the statue, brushing away the dust from the misplaced scrape. Not too deep. He could remedy the fault.

Another snatch of conversation. *Deuce take it!* He'd given explicit instructions no one but himself should approach the folly. When a certain voice drifted up to him more clearly, he rolled his eyes. He'd heard that one before, defying him to his face.

Had the Wyndham chit any idea with whom she was dealing?

There was no need to look out the window to confirm his suspicions. Yet his feet carried him there, and when he could see nothing, he dropped his chisel on the workbench and headed up to the roof.

It was a fine day. He supposed he couldn't blame anyone for choosing to be outside in it, but with gardens covering twenty acres and a park extending a good hundred, there were plenty of other places where people could be.

He bent over the parapet to see what was happening below but swayed forward as the nausea took him again. As he did each time he came up here, he experienced the pull of the ground as an irresistible force, compelling him to leap out into oblivion.

No. At least, not until the statue was finished, and Polly able to hold her own amongst her peers. But she could only do so if Miss Galatea Wyndham stopped being so damned soft on her.

He would have to confront the disturbers of his peace. Hal dragged himself down the spiral staircase of the tower and eventually burst out into the sunlight at its foot. Locking the door with trembling fingers, he crunched and slithered down the steps, took a deep breath at the bottom, and strode around the base of the tower.

"Lord Ansford. Good morning, and a most pleasant one it is too. Say hello to your papa, Polly."

He shifted his gaze from Miss Wyndham's face and found his daughter gazing up at him with gray eyes the match of her mother's. The stabbing ache in his gut intensified cruelly.

Anger was the best refuge against the pain.

"Miss Wyndham," he snapped, "Once again you trample on my rules and violate my privacy. You must learn—"

"Polly, your father needs a drink of water. Pray run along to Cook and fetch some. Walk nicely as I've taught you and be careful not to spill it."

Hal glowered as his daughter hurtled off toward the house, kicking her heels up behind her. No one ever interrupted him mid-sentence. Fury warred with astonishment.

"Miss Wyndham, I'm not in the least bit thirsty. Why—"

"Sir, you are pale and trembling, as if you've seen a ghost. Indeed, you rather resemble one. Did you know you were covered in dust?"

He started to brush at his chest but stopped himself. Why should he care what he looked like in his own home, on his own estate?

The chit's eyes followed the movement of his hand, before locking defiantly on his face. She tilted her chin. "I assume you are come to ring a peal over me for approaching your horrible folly tower. That's why I sent Polly away. To be disrespectful to me in front of the child would undermine my authority."

It was an effort not to gape like a fish at this assertion and the temerity of its author. "Surely you are aware, Miss Wyndham," he snarled, quaking with fury, "the folly and its environs are out of bounds to all but myself?"

"I thought we'd managed to keep a respectful distance away. We're sketching the tower, you see. I'm teaching Polly how to work with pencils, and the grayness of the stone made it an admirable subject. There seems to be a lot of holes between the stones, my lord. I can't help but wonder if rain is eroding the ash away, or charcoal, or whatever the dark stuff is that's been mixed in with the mortar."

"Ash? Be damned to ash! Stop trying to wriggle off the hook, Miss Wyndham—it will not do."

Her half-smile faltered, and he recognized only too well the expression of steely determination lurking in her velvet-brown eyes.

"If you are so averse to the distant sound of muted voices—for we didn't exactly shout while we were sketching—maybe you could put something in your ears, so you are not disturbed?"

Hal stared at his opponent. And stared some more. A peculiar sensation rose from the pit of his stomach to his diaphragm.

It was so unfamiliar, he almost forgot his vow of rigid emotional control. No—he must never laugh, particularly not in front of this defiant little minx.

"Thank you for the suggestion," he replied with some effort, "but it's much easier if you simply keep away from my folly. And while we're on the subject of your inability to do as you're told, I'd like to know what you mean by stealing books from my library. What need have you of a book on the decoration of Grecian urns, pray? I think a nine-year-old girl too young to be examining images of naked fornication, don't you?"

He hid the glow of triumph that shot through him. From the color in her cheeks, he'd found a way to rattle the chit.

"I didn't mean to defy you, sir. I merely thought perhaps, so long as I didn't disturb you, it would be acceptable for me to make use of so valuable a resource in our lessons."

Hal regarded his antagonist. It was a long time since anyone had dared to stand up to him. The last perpetrator of this heinous crime had been Mary, but she had more justification than this young stranger.

How unlike Mary she was, not tall and elegant but of middling height, with a girlish heart-shaped face and shining brown curls to frame it. She was perhaps somewhat thinner than he would have wished, but it was not to be wondered at, considering the difficulties she and her mother had been through. He resisted the urge to tell her to eat more freely from his table and build herself up, filling out those promising curves.

Wait—what was he thinking?

"My lord, are you all right?"

He waved a dismissive hand. "I'm fine, don't fuss."

Immediately she seized him by the arm and made him sit down on the bottom step of the folly's staircase.

"You're dizzy and hot. I'm sorry, it's a bit dirty to make

you sit here—there's a lot of dark dust. I fear the foundations of your folly may be crumbling, sir."

Amen to that. He was helpless in the face of so much solicitude.

Damn this vertigo! He was one of the most successful, the most important gentlemen in this half of the county and he didn't need a nursemaid. Yet here he was, bemused, baited, and nearly bested by someone he'd barely met.

To his chagrin, Polly returned, walking stiffly across the grass so as not to spill a single drop of the water she'd brought him. Wonderful. Now his daughter was going to be witness to his weakness too.

Polly's fingers brushed his as she handed him the glass, and he spilled some water, unused to the touch of a small, warm hand.

Miss Wyndham crouched beside him, shading her eyes and examining him closely. "I think," she stated, "you spend too much time in darkness and not enough in the health-giving daylight. I've seen the lamps lit in the folly at night when I can't sleep and have to walk about a bit. You would benefit from proper sleep and a good tonic. I can make you a decoction of St. John's Wort if you like. There's plenty growing hereabouts. I'd enjoy making it up for you."

"Ah." He nodded his understanding. One of the missing books had been an herbal, an ancient volume from the days of Queen Bess. "You fancy making potions and trying them out on me. You'll not find me a good subject, and I take exception to being experimented on."

She'd probably poison him, despite having the best of intentions. Not that he had much reason to continue on in this mortal coil, but it would be a shame if she were punished for removing him from it.

"You should be sure to get a proper amount of sleep. Go to bed with the nightingale and rise with the lark."

Clearly, she'd also taken a volume of Shakespeare's tragedies from his shelves. "You forget, it is my daughter you are supposed to be teaching, not myself."

His eyes flicked to Polly. She was a good deal grown since the last time he'd appraised her properly. His gaze roved back to Miss Wyndham.

Why was she concerned for his well-being when he'd already shown himself to have no interest in either her person or her opinions? It had been such a long time since his entrance into any meaningful discourse with an equal, he'd forgotten how to read between the lines.

He should do what he normally did in such situations. Regard his foe with casual disdain, refuse to respond to their barbs, and wait until they gave up and went away. But he was acutely aware of Polly watching him, rendering him awkward.

Miss Wyndham continued to regard him with a questioning gaze, but a glance past his shoulder at the folly betrayed her.

So that was it, was it? She pretended to offer him compassion but what she really wanted was to expose his secrets.

"You want to know what I do in there all night. Unfortunately for you, Miss Wyndham, I won't satisfy your curiosity. You'll never know what—if anything—I have to hide. Don't think to question the servants. They know nothing, and even if they did, they're all loyal to me."

Hal became aware of Polly staring at him. Damn. Despite himself, he was reacting to Miss Wyndham. He shouldn't give a fig what she, or his daughter, thought about him.

"My child," he said, testing the words on his tongue, "run along and find your nurse. Miss Wyndham and I need to speak alone."

Polly obediently took his empty glass and skipped back to the house while Miss Wyndham pushed herself upright.

A gentleman would have assisted her, but what cared he for such niceties? He tried not to care about anything much anymore. Except making sure Polly could protect herself from the gossips.

He, too, got to his feet and took a pace forward, allowing his height to dominate the young woman, knowing how others in the past had found his stature intimidating. To his surprise, she stood her ground, regarding him with a quizzical expression.

"I imagine you've sent Polly away so you can cross swords with me again."

Was she actually enjoying this? He needed to put a period to this conversation.

"That would take more effort than I can be bothered to summon," he drawled. "No, I wanted to make sure we understood one another."

"My lord, I don't presume to understand you, and I'm quite certain you don't understand me."

"Merely a figure of speech, Miss Wyndham. I have a great deal to say about your attitude toward educating Polly, but to make sure you remember it, I'll write some points down in a note."

He waited, but she showed no inclination to leave. "Was there something else you wished to say?" he inquired, with a sigh of resignation.

A flush suffused her cheeks. She could be quite pretty—if she weren't so annoying. Then he divined her thoughts, and an icy hand closed around his heart. Confound it, was she the same as the rest of them, all the tabbies and gossips, the people who thought he'd done away with Mary? Or maybe she was more charitable in her imaginings and believed he was keeping his wife locked up somewhere in punishment for some misdemeanor, or that she'd run mad and was now incarcerated in the tower.

Disappointment mingled with anger and without thinking, he took hold of her and pulled her close until she had to bend her neck to look up at him. Her face a mask of shock, she tried to pull away, but he refused to release her. His fingers dug into the soft flesh of her arms, making him aware of the delicate bones beneath. He was being a brute, but he couldn't help himself.

"Now listen to me, Galatea Wyndham," he growled. "There are no skeletons in any of my closets, however hard you search. My wife is truly dead and lies in the crypt beneath Foxleaze. I'm not using the folly as a laboratory to give animation back to her corpse like Victor Frankenstein." At her blink, he added wearily, "You look amazed. You never expected me to have any modern literature in my collection, I imagine."

She has no idea what kind of a man I am. None at all. He shook his head. "I don't know what ideas your fevered imagination may have conjured up, but none of them comes near the truth."

Her eyes widened, and she shivered in his grasp. He released her instantly, hating himself for being the cause of her horrified expression, and wondered if there was any way of summoning up a reassuring grin.

He tried it, and she took two steps backward.

"Pray do not grimace at me. I promise I'm not in the least bit ungrateful for all the kindnesses you have bestowed on us, but your manners are deplorable."

He gasped, but she carried on regardless.

"I know I should not say this to my benefactor—"

"Undoubtedly."

"Lest you take offense and turn us out. But I thought you needed to know my mama is most upset by your attitude and that you're making an enemy of Polly with your aloofness and your rigid rules. The girl needs a father, sir, and it is your duty, *your duty*—but I can see in your face I'm wasting my time. You might as well be deaf and blind, for all the notice you take of anybody."

Having delivered that volley, she spun on her heel, hastily gathered up her sketchbooks and pencils, and headed back to the house.

Turning away, Hal thrust his hands behind his back and stalked down the grassy slope toward the lake. A coot scudded away as he approached the bank and he gazed down at the rippled water until the surface settled. Seeing his reflection, framed by billowing white clouds and azure sky, Hal leaned down and peered more closely.

The Wyndham chit was right to be afraid, damn her. He looked debauched, with his lank locks and shadowed eyes. No wonder people imagined terrible things about him. But maybe it was for the best, for on the whole it kept them away, and solitude was what he craved more than anything.

He would have to find a way to assert his will over the flighty Miss Wyndham, or his life was going to become a great deal more difficult. The simplest solution would be to get rid of the women. He'd find them somewhere else to live, of course, and make sure they had whatever they needed.

But he'd better set about it soon before they became too attached to their new home—or to Polly. He would have a word with Lynch this afternoon and see what could be done.

Chapter 10

Though a beautifully sunny day outside, Tia had elected to spend at least part of it within, penning a letter to her old schoolfriend Lucy. The past week had been difficult, and she was desperate to unburden herself to someone who knew about Lord Ansford. He'd been behaving most oddly, and she couldn't tell if it was a good sign or quite the opposite.

Much to her surprise, he'd eventually made the acquaintance of Mama but had only exchanged the briefest of greetings with her. He was occasionally to be found in one of the downstairs rooms in the middle of the house, a place once used as a drawing room, mayhap, in the days when Foxleaze Abbey had welcomed guests. The papers were brought to him there and when he'd finished with them, he would generally disappear, leaving them for the Wyndhams to peruse at their leisure.

On a couple of occasions, Ansford had stayed late reading and had actually been quite polite when they burst in on him unawares. Tia almost imagined he might have hung back deliberately in order to see them.

He seemed different. It took her some time to realize it was because he had donned a white shirt and cravat instead of his usual black. Was he trying to lull her into a false sense of security by making himself more presentable? Surely, she hadn't already pierced his armor of indifference?

Unfortunately, Polly had become sullener after the incident outside the folly. Maybe—and not without reason—the child thought her papa would take more of an interest in her, now he'd been forced to speak to her. Her disappointment was palpable, and it was as much as Tia could do to get her to work at all or indulge in conversation.

"I don't know what to make of the man," she wrote to her friend. *"I'm sure there is much good in him, only he casts a pall of misery about him wherever he goes. Pray, ask your husband if his old friend has always been so morose, or if his wife's death has wrought this change in him."*

She paused and gazed out the window. She'd done something utterly ridiculous the other day. So foolish, in fact, she had to force herself to admit it to Lucy.

"Having a notion the baroness might still be alive and imprisoned in the forbidden folly, I went to see if I could determine whether or not her body lay in her tomb. Of course, I could never have pushed that great stone lid off, but I was just thinking about it when Lord Ansford came upon me."

She quivered with embarrassment at the memory. She'd told him she was merely perusing the charming Fifteenth century carvings.

"I fear he divined my purpose. He gave me that look of his, when his blue eyes turn almost black, and his brows knit together in disapproval. He just told me to keep away and loomed there until I left. Can you imagine anything more frustrating? A man who lays down the law but gives no good reason."

She paused in her writing, recalling the expression on Ansford's face. He'd nodded to himself as he dismissed her from the vault, as if he'd made his mind up about something. She wasn't sure she wanted to know what it was.

Mama bustled in. "Tia, we have some post. One is an invitation to dine with the Douglas family of Amesbury."

Tia put down her pen and blew on the wet ink before turning to her mother. "An invitation? How splendid."

More than splendid, in truth. She could barely recall the last time she and Mama had attended any social engagement. Her father's funeral had been the last time they'd seen all their friends and family. It hadn't taken long for many of those people to abandon the Wyndham ladies when the extent of their debts was known. Thank goodness for Lucy and the Duke of Finchingfield.

Thank goodness for Lord Ansford too. No matter how pathetic an excuse for a gentleman he might be, he had, nonetheless, rescued them from the worst of situations.

"Yes," Mama went on, "Ansford gave it to me this morning. Or should I say, sent it up with a footman."

"He didn't reply himself?"

"Oh no. He won't be going. You know he hates society."

Tia's charitable thoughts of Lord Ansford lost some of their gloss. "The Douglas family will be disappointed when they learn it's only us."

"It's a beginning, Tia. Mourning affects people differently. One day he may find confidence enough to accompany us."

Tia snorted. "I don't think confidence is what he lacks, Mama. He is too bullheaded to change his mind about anything."

She glanced toward the window. June was now in progress, and despite recent rain, the prospect for the day was promising. Swallows swooped low above the grass while swifts screamed overhead, performing their aerial chases and dives. It was so beautiful. She mustn't let anything spoil her enjoyment of it.

"Mama, am I too hard on Lord Ansford? I wouldn't want to endanger our position here." Whatever frustrations she might have with the owner of Foxleaze, whatever grim secrets the place might harbor, she would miss it sorely if they were forced to leave.

"I don't think you mean to goad him," her mother replied, giving her a level look. "Although I agree he often deserves it. You're not quite your old self yet. The hardships you've been through have taken their toll, and you've witnessed the kind of suffering a young gentlewoman ought never to see. I think you're smarting from your wounds and need to strike out. Ansford, although guiltless of your original pain, has become your scapegoat. I suggest you're sensitive to his faults because you take them personally—at a time when you need a boost to your confidence, his indifferent behavior has the opposite effect."

Tia chewed on her lip. This last was almost certainly true, though she hated to admit it. She threw her head back and forced a laugh. "Mama, how perceptive you've become."

"More than you know, my dear, more than you know. Now, shall we plunder the late baroness's collection of the Lady's Magazine? We can hunt for ideas on what to wear for our evening out."

"They're in the morning room, are they not? Surely Ansford's 'Rules' dictate that room should stay shut up?"

Mama rolled her eyes. "I was planning on borrowing a few copies and bringing them back to our sitting room. Or we could read them here."

A frisson of excitement skittered up Tia's spine. It was ridiculous they shouldn't be allowed to use the morning room. It only needed the covers to be whisked off and shaken to make the place perfectly habitable. Polly could come and join them—there was a card table, a pianoforte, a splendid collection of ladies' magazines and journals, and a large, modern window admitting more daylight than any other in the building.

Ansford wouldn't like it if they opened up the morning room.

So, I won't bother to ask him.

Chapter 11

Hal stalked across the Turkish carpet and gazed out the study window. The Wyndhams were still here. If Lynch hadn't contracted that damn quinsy, he'd have been rid of them by now.

Of course, he could have dealt with the matter himself, but it would mean he'd have to face up to them. Talking was so awkward. The more one spoke, the more entangled one became in the conversation, and he hated the impression of being trapped.

An image of Galatea's beautiful, bright face swam before his mind's eye. She'd have told him straight what she thought of him for so heinous an act of betrayal. He couldn't help but applaud her courage in standing up to him, even when in his darkest mood.

He drummed his fingers on the stone windowsill. He wouldn't have been able to remove the Wyndhams from Foxleaze immediately in any case, as he'd not yet decided how close, or how far away, their new home needed to be. He was their benefactor, after all, and would have to continue dealing with their business issues.

So, in the interim, he would simply have to cope with the bloodless battle going on between himself and Miss Wyndham-she with her desire to amend his manners and behavior, and he equally determined to change nothing.

Hal knew she disapproved of his appearance. Her lips flattened when they encountered one another, and she always ran her eyes over his black-clad form. Well, he'd made a concession by wearing a white shirt and cravat. That was all, for he was in mourning and only *he* would decide when to come out of it.

He'd seen her eyeing his hair too. Perhaps she believed, because it was often damp, he'd combed oil into it. This was not the case, of course—where was the point in putting pomade on one's hair if one went for a bracing swim every day? It would be a waste of money.

He didn't care what she thought of his appearance. Although the glimpse of himself in the lake the other day had given him pause for thought.

Hal stroked his chin. When had he last accepted a shave? He couldn't remember. And the beard—if he intended to keep it—needed a trim, or it would become as straggly as his hair.

Not that it mattered.

It was warm, standing here with the rectangular glass panes intensifying the sunlight. If he were in the folly— where he ought to be currently—he'd be unaware of either the light or the warmth. He really ought to go and get on with his project.

Instead, his fingers reached for the window catch. This was a sash window, and he couldn't recall the last time he'd opened it. The sound of the lead weights moving down inside the frame grated in his head, but it was worth it for the sweet air he sucked into his lungs.

A swallow skidded past, and moments later he heard the faint peeping of chicks from a nest nearby. Mary had always loved summer here, and so had he. The place was full of teeming life, with the lowing of cattle in the distant meadows, birds frantically proclaiming their territories, and the bees buzzing around the bobbing flower-heads.

Once he used to enjoy watching Polly from this window— she'd emerge onto the grass trailing a skipping rope, and she'd try to beat her previous total of jumps, counting out to herself under her breath. It was amusing when she became entangled and had to start again.

But nothing amused him now.

Turning away from the window, Hal clenched his teeth against the memories and the pain. Everything had changed so much in the past three years. There was no way of reversing the clock, of recapturing his lost happiness.

But he could make at least one change. The weather was balmy, after all—they'd already reached midsummer, and it wouldn't be long before the blazing days of August arrived. Did he truly want to be sweltering under long hair and a beard?

A pull on the bell-rope brought his footman, Aldergate, to the door.

"Find Symons, will you? Tell him I'd like a shave."

Was that an expression of triumph on the footman's face? Surely a decision to shave wasn't *that* significant an event?

A short while later, Hal was settled in the chair in front of his dressing table. He could see Symon's face in the mirror as the man placed a towel around his shoulders. Like Aldergate, he seemed excessively cheerful today.

"Mrs. and Miss Wyndham have opened up the morning room, sir, and settled themselves down to their needlework because the light there at this time of day is exceedingly good. Or so they informed me."

Hal's reflection scowled at him. How dare they open a room in his house without his express permission? Or that of Mrs. Dunne? Had the irksome Miss Wyndham found a way to compel the servants to do her bidding?

Infuriating. But Hal shouldn't admit to it, because being angry suggested he cared.

He'd made up his mind long ago to care a good deal less than he used to.

It hurt too much.

All the same, as soon as his shave was complete, he set off for the morning room to express his displeasure, but the scene before him brought him up short.

The Wyndhams had shifted the sofa around and now sat facing the window, accompanied by Polly on a small footstool. All three were absorbed in their tasks. Polly was trimming an old bonnet, tongue clenched between her teeth in concentration. Mrs. Wyndham was crocheting with hairpins, and Galatea embroidered a thin square of lawn. She gazed down at her needlework frame, her long dark lashes caressing porcelain cheeks, her luscious mouth pursed in concentration.

She was so lovely, his heart lurched.

Hal shook away his inappropriate, unwelcome response. But he couldn't help continuing to observe her. The light was so clear today, it picked out every curl of her shining hair, every fold of her sprigged muslin dress, the delicate curve of her shoulders, and the tempting swell of her breasts.

She seemed as if posed for a portrait, but if he attempted to capture the moment, he'd need to fetch his drawing things. By the time he'd done that, the moment would have passed. Better to stand quietly in the doorway and commit the sight to memory while he waited for someone to notice his presence, allowing him to penetrate the bubble of domesticity.

Miss Wyndham beamed to herself, sucked in a breath, and hummed a few bars of what sounded like a sea shanty. When her sweet voice broke out in song, her mother and Polly laid aside their work to watch and listen. There was a chorus, which Polly, ever a bright child, quickly picked up, and soon all three were raising their heads and adjuring the spirits of Foxleaze to, 'Haul away the bow-line, the bowline haul.'

Something snapped inside Hal, propelling him into the room in a blaze of fury.

"Silence!" he roared. "Don't you know this is a house of mourning? I will *not* have common sea shanties sung here. You will desist at once or leave now."

Chapter 12

A hiccupping sob from Polly broke the stunned silence following Lord Ansford's outburst. As Mama put a comforting arm about the girl's shoulders, Tia marched the irate baron out of the room, slamming the door shut behind her.

"I presume you intend to apologize." His blue eyes glittered with anger, his voice harsh.

He expected *her* to say sorry? He'd reduced his daughter to tears, insulted her and her mother and threatened to throw them all out. The urge to slap Lord Ansford's maddeningly handsome—and, she suddenly noticed, fashionably beardless—face was almost overwhelming.

"My lord," she began, battling to keep her tone low and even, "we were not aware singing was forbidden. Had I known you meant to deny us every pleasure known to humankind, I'd have stayed in the poorhouse. At least I'd have been able to do some good for the children there."

Ansford caught her by the arm and gave her a light shake. "Miss Wyndham," he snapped, his voice hard, unyielding. "My house, my rules. There's been no music here since Lady Mary died. I find I much prefer the quiet."

"Must there never be music again?" Tia was very aware of the pressure of his warm fingers on her upper arms. He was close enough for her to recognize the fury emanating from his body.

"If I decree it, yes."

"And Polly is never to touch the pianoforte, or hum a melody? How will she fare in the drawing rooms of the *ton*? How can she attract a husband if she is unable to play?

Would you deny her the chance for future happiness, of future security?"

His fingers tightened, forcing into Tia's mind all the rumors about the baron, all the cruel things he was considered capable of doing. He wouldn't hurt her, surely? Nonetheless, she went completely rigid, fearing she'd said too much.

"I'm trying to help the child," Ansford persisted. "She needs to be impenetrable. I don't want her to care for anyone so much she can't bear to be parted from them, and I don't want her to suffer the pain of a loss so great she can barely live with herself. I don't want her to lose a loved one and wish it should have been her who was taken rather than the one robbed of life many years too soon."

Like a physical touch, his eyes raked her face, his gaze dark with anger, his lips trembling with the effort to quell the rage.

The man revealed a great deal more about himself than he had about his plans for Polly. Tia's fury ebbed away as she relaxed in his grasp.

"You forget, sir, I too have loved and lost. I lost a sister before I lost my father. Both were taken away far too young. I continue to grieve for them, in my own way. Mama and I have faced great hardship and seen all safety and security stripped away from us, yet we've never given up hope. We've never given up seeking whatever happiness life has to offer." It was hard to keep her voice from quavering at the remembered misery and loss.

"I'm sorry for your suffering, truly I am, but you bring it all on yourself. The time for mourning has passed, and you must learn to live again. If not for yourself, for Polly. Do you want her to be a timid mouse all her life, forever afraid to enjoy herself, or make music or laugh for fear of censure? No, I can't believe you do. You were a great man once, sir. You can be that man again. But don't leave it too late, or you'll find there is nothing left of him."

Ansford's fingers slipped down to her elbows. They were standing breast to breast now, two foes locked in mortal combat, with words for swords and each with their own pride and stubbornness to shield them.

Tia's eyes slid from the man's freshly shaven chin to his white cravat, his broad chest heaving with the strength of his anger, the black, featureless clothing that signaled to everybody he was dead to the world.

And found herself fervently wishing it were otherwise. What if those hands were to draw her closer, the strong arms to cradle her against his firm chest, the warm fingers to stroke her hair and tell her it was all right, that everything was going to be well?

Comfort, indeed. Something she had not, until this moment, known she either needed or desired.

She gulped, and the tears brimmed up. This could not be allowed to happen. Wrenching herself from Ansford's grasp, she pushed past him.

"I'm sorry, my lord. I've said too much. Forgive me. You don't need to send Polly away, for I promise there will be no more singing at Foxleaze."

He reached for her, but she evaded him.

"Miss Wyndham, wait. Please, Galatea!"

She ran down the echoing passageway, blinded by tears. The encounter had opened old wounds. Why waste any more time on Henry Pelham, eighth Baron Ansford? He was beyond her help. He was beyond the help of anybody.

The sound of hurrying feet pursued her. He mustn't see he'd made her cry. She burst into the entrance hall, ran up the stairs, thought briefly of hiding behind the suit of armor, and decided to make for her bedchamber. Her adversary wouldn't follow her there.

Ansford would have no wish to entertain his staff by pursuing her through the whole length of the house, only to be left locked out and looking foolish before her door.

Damn, the man was fast when he wanted to be. He caught up with her at the top of the stairs, seized her arm, and steered her wordlessly through the connecting door and into his wing of the house. She found herself being frog-marched down a passageway, around a corner, and eventually into the corridor that held the library. Exactly what he intended to do with her, she'd no idea. Had she left it too late to scream?

Next minute, they were in his study, with the door shut behind them. She had to hope he hadn't really murdered his wife in a fit of rage.

He held her at arm's length, and she raised a defiant chin to him. With any luck, he'd never know how close to despair he'd driven her.

"Galatea, don't run away from me." His voice was soft and earnest. "I'd never harm you, trust me. I may be a hollow shell of a man, but I've not lost my humanity. I'll argue with you, yes, and I have every right—you stubbornly refuse to understand me, or why I live by the rules I do. It makes me angry. It would make anyone angry. But I beg you, don't be frightened of me and don't let me hurt you. I'm not worth it."

"I'm not crying, and I'm not afraid," she lied. "I have wounds of my own to deal with, and sometimes they get the better of me. That is all."

"I'm sorry. I must try to curb my temper. It has always been a failing of mine. I had thought I no longer cared enough to be angry about anything, but no matter. Come, let us sheathe our weapons and be friends, or at least call a truce. I suppose you will now tell me to make amends to Polly. As for music, I'll consider the points you've made."

Hope sprang to life, and Tia almost grinned. This was the first time Ansford had offered to consider making a concession. And he'd spoken more in the last fifteen minutes, revealed more of his true character than he had in the last month.

To her astonishment, he embraced her, his hands awkward and shy. He pressed her only lightly against his chest, but it was long enough for her to notice the softness of his clothing and the firmness of the muscles flexing beneath it. His head bent close to hers, long hair brushing her cheek.

She sniffed. And sniffed again. "My lord," she said as he released her, "I hope you won't think me rude, but you smell most peculiar."

"I beg your pardon?" The dark brows shot up.

"If I didn't know better, I'd say your hair smelled of pondweed."

"Ah, Miss Wyndham is herself again," he retorted, taking her hand.

An instant connection throbbed between them. Had he felt it too?

If he were to try that embrace again, she'd make it work much better. And last considerably longer.

Hal's blue eyes glittered. Had he divined her thoughts? She hoped not.

"You really are the most critical female I've ever met. Let us agree I'll never come up to your exacting standards and you won't come up to mine. I can promise you no more comforting embraces if all you're going to do is make personal remarks. I've been swimming in the river, as I do virtually every day. My valet neglected to tell me it made my hair smell of pondweed. Would the application of a perfumed oil satisfy you? Or perhaps a simple rinse in rosemary-water?"

Obviously not offended, he was looking happy now, sporting the first true smile he'd given her. His fingers caressed her wrist, sending a jolt of sensation right up her arm. What allure this man possessed. God forbid he ever chose to use his power.

"That might indeed serve." She was desperate now to break the spell he'd cast on her. "Although it badly needs cutting too. As does Polly's. Her maid Paulet is good at styling but has an unsteady hand when it comes to scissors."

What was she prattling on about? She needed to get out of here before she uttered something completely idiotic.

"Granted. I bow to your superior knowledge, Miss Wyndham. If you do a good job on Polly, you may cut my hair as well, in whatever way it pleases you."

Tempting. Extremely tempting. It was a frightful mess. "You jest with me, sir."

The fingers on her wrist stilled, but his expression didn't change. She wondered if he was even aware of stroking her.

"I'm not known for my jokes, Galatea." He rolled her name around on his tongue as if tasting it and finding it sweet. His eyes held hers and the air between them crackled like summer lightning.

Tia's mind went blank. Damn the man for undermining her certainties and prejudice. He was a bad-tempered boor. She hated him, and the last thing she needed was to fall under his spell. She shook his hand away.

"No sir, it would be most improper. What do I know of styling a gentleman's hair? I'd make you into a scarecrow or a . . . a Frankenstein monster and you wouldn't thank me for it. I must go now and check on Polly. Will you come back with me and apologize?"

He edged away and opened the door for her. His voice sounded hollow as he replied, "You're quite right. I'll order Polly a new doll and some fabric to sew clothes for it. Will that make her happy?"

Tia paused on the threshold and gave him a helpless look. Did he genuinely not know what Polly needed? Could he not even make a pretense at affection for his daughter? Even the briefest of hugs from her papa would do wonders for the girl, as would a ride on those broad shoulders.

Or even just a smile.

"Lord Ansford," she returned stiffly, "a doll would distract her, but it's a cowardly solution. Come and talk to her, calm her, soothe her. Be a father to her, sir. It's all I ask."

With that, she hurried away from him and clattered down the stairs into the cloisters. Choosing the archway as the quickest path to freedom and the air she so much needed, she headed into the sunshine and reveled in its warmth while she willed her heart to a more comfortable beat.

Her eye was drawn to the folly in the distance, the tall, dark edifice that embodied Lord Ansford's stubbornness and his pride.

She lifted her chin. One day she would breach its walls and discover its secrets, at which point she would finally have power over its owner.

Enough to begin the process of exorcising the spirit that haunted him.

Chapter 13

Sir Kennet Douglas bent over Tia's hand before ushering her into his spacious drawing room, the behavior of a true gentleman.

So, this is what it's like to be treated like a lady.

Tia tried to remember the last time she and Mama had been welcomed with such polite cordiality. For certain, not since before Papa's death.

She felt like a princess in her new evening gown of cream silk, a finer garment than anything she'd ever had before, thanks to Lord Ansford's generosity. She'd even borrowed a set of the late baroness's pearls, also a sign of his beneficence.

Perhaps it was his way of apologizing for embarrassing his new relations by not accompanying them to this dinner party. He hadn't given them a valid excuse to offer Sir Kennet and Lady Douglas, so Tia had to fabricate a tale about his fears he, like his steward, might have the quinsy.

How often was she going to have to lie, to cover Ansford's selfish thoughtlessness?

Further introductions were made to Mr. Peel and his wife, and next to Mr. Brooks and his good lady. These gentlemen, as Tia was to discover, were the Members of Parliament for Chippenham and she soon found herself conversing with the former about Lord Ansford.

She should have expected it since gossip loved a recluse. Especially one who might have contributed to his wife's death.

Mr. Brooks, however, was fastidious in his efforts not to mention any slanderous tittle-tattle. "He was a bit of a radical in his day. A young hothead, even. He made a fair few enemies when he opposed the Corn Laws, enemies amongst his own kind."

"Well, I think it good he championed the poor," Mrs. Brooks interjected from her side of the dining table. "If that mob had carried out their threats to attack Parliament, he would have been one of the few politicians to be spared."

A younger gentleman, by the name of Mr. Londis, claimed to have been in the capital during the riots and proceeded to tell some hair-raising stories about what he'd seen, until silenced by the arrival of dessert.

The subject of Ansford was broached again later when the company was seated in the music room. Mr. Brooks, who seemed to have taken Tia under his wing, commented, "Ansford was halfway to being hailed as a popular hero. Had he not crumbled when his wife died, who knows what he might have become?"

Tia pondered the question. The Ansford she knew had nothing of the savior about him. "I don't think being a hero of the populace is a good way to progress a political career, is it? Not after what happened in France last century."

"I agree." This from Mr. Londis, who had taken up position beside the sofa while Lady Douglas settled herself at the pianoforte. "Almost anyone who appears to support the poor folk is liable to be called a Jacobin. And if you have anything to say to the distress caused in manufacturing towns by the introduction of new machinery, you are labeled a Luddite. It doesn't do to champion the lesser man."

But someone had to. Was that why Ansford had rescued herself and Mama from the poorhouse? Because he understood the suffering to be found there? Perhaps he was still capable of being altruistic about matters of great importance but could no longer bring himself to care about small issues closer to home.

Mama gave a light laugh. "Listen to us, joining in a discussion on political opinions. That I even consider myself entitled to have an opinion is due to Lord Ansford. So many different newspapers and journals are delivered to his door. I declare I'd have no idea at all what a Jacobin or a Luddite might be, had I not read the papers when he was finished with them."

Another good point in our benefactor's favor, I suppose. The man is well-read.

Mr. Londis leaned down and coughed politely. "Now, we don't want to bore you ladies with our conversation, do we, Brooks? The time for entertainment has come upon us. Do you play, Miss Wyndham?"

Yes, she had once played, a little. But the pianoforte at Foxleaze was out of bounds. "I fear my skills are rather rusty, sir," she replied, with what she hoped was a gracious expression.

"Oh, no one's a critic here. Lady Douglas plays quite abominably," he whispered, "and no one minds at all. Surely, you must play something. Allow me to bring you a sheaf of tunes once her ladyship has finished her piece."

As everyone fell silent to listen to Lady Douglas's genuinely awful but enthusiastic performance, Tia's thoughts strayed again to Ansford. He seemed well thought of here, so whence came the vicious rumors about his wife's death? His political opponents? Perhaps wealthy landowners who didn't much care for his opposition to the Corn Laws? Rich industrialists, who objected to his comments about the riots? Or, more likely, the wives of such men?

The idea of Ansford being a political firebrand fascinated her. She could well believe it, as she'd seen passion burst out from behind his cold, indifferent exterior. But the passion had only taken the form of anger so far. What would it be like if transmuted into something more positive?

Love, for instance.

She opened her fan and wafted it rapidly in front of her burning face. From where had that thought come?

Aware of Mr. Londis's eyes on her, she glanced up. With a charming smile, he asked, *sotto voce,* "Might I have one of the windows opened for you?"

She returned his smile but shook her head. As she composed herself to listen politely to the music, she couldn't help but think Mr. Londis, or his friend, the shy Mr. Leigh, were exactly the sort of gentlemen with whom she should be spending more time. These were the sort of men she should be pursuing with a view to marriage.

Her perplexing protector must be excised from her mind. She was here to enjoy herself. Ansford, that dismal scourge of everything enjoyable, could just sink into his mire of melancholy, for all she cared.

So long as he didn't suck his daughter down with him.

Chapter 14

After the excitements of the previous day, Tia was late down to breakfast, but despite being tired, she was in an ebullient mood.

So was Mama. "What a pleasant evening. I can't remember the last time we enjoyed such good company and excellent food. I don't mean to decry Ansford's hospitality of course—his table is of the finest, but I find his company somewhat . . . lowering."

Tia nodded her agreement. When Ansford entered a room, his presence made the air hang heavy, and it became hard to breathe. But he was improving.

Slightly.

By giving her a piece of his mind the other day, he'd also given her a window into his soul. And he'd made a halting apology to Mama for exploding at them in the morning room. He was a long way from being reformed, however.

"Sir Kennet Douglas is quite charming, is he not?" Mama continued.

"A true gentleman, although he couldn't hide his disappointment at Ansford's absence." Tia helped herself to another muffin. "I have to say, I'm glad Ansford didn't come. He'd have cast a dark shadow across everything."

Mama tutted and waved her napkin. "Hush, you never know where he might be lurking. You wouldn't want him to overhear that kind of remark."

Actually, I would. It might do him good.

Before she could respond, a scrabbling noise erupted from the floor. Mama pushed her chair back in alarm and

Tia peered beneath the table, in time to see a short furry tail disappear behind her mother's skirts.

"Oh." She sat upright again. "It's Polly's kitten. Not a rat, at least."

"A kitten at the breakfast table? How shocking. Wherever has that come from?"

"Don't worry. You remember last week when Ansford shouted at us and upset Polly?"

Mama nodded.

"While I remonstrated with the baron, you took Polly to the barn to see the farm cat's litter to cheer her up. Well, the sly little vixen must have put a kitten in her pocket when your back was turned. I discovered it later in the schoolroom trying to put its paw in the inkwell, but I hadn't the heart to punish Polly. She needs something to love, and if her papa won't allow her to love him—"

"Good morning Mrs. Wyndham, Miss Wyndham."

Tia's teacup shook in her hand, her body heavy as lead. Had Ansford overheard her?

She self-consciously muttered a reply and tried not to stare as he took a place at the table. Aldergate appeared immediately to take his order of spiced ham, coddled eggs with field mushrooms, and his 'special tea.' A copy of *The Morning Post* appeared as if by magic at Ansford's elbow, along with a small Wedgwood teapot. He peered inside, gave the tea a swirl, and set it down again.

His unexpected presence at the breakfast table killed all conversation. Tia struggled to continue with her breakfast and behave as if nothing truly momentous had occurred.

Ansford, joining them for breakfast? Being sociable? *Unheard of.*

"How was dinner at the Douglas mansion?" he inquired.

Mama shot Tia an astonished glance. "Why, it was most pleasant. We were warmly welcomed and introduced to several people, including Mr. Peel, Mr. Brooks and his wife, and Mr. Leigh. Lady Douglas entertained us on the pianoforte. We had a delicious white soup, didn't we, Tia? And the pork was superlative."

Mama coughed and looked self-conscious. Tia understood how hard it was to talk to Ansford when he offered no response.

His meal was served to him. He nodded his thanks, then turned his startling blue gaze on Tia. She swallowed hard and lowered her eyes.

"Miss Wyndham, I trust you enjoyed yourself as well?"

"I did, my lord. Thank you." She wanted to add, *so would you have, if you could have bestirred yourself to come,* but she knew exactly how he'd react.

She waited for him to pick up his newspaper and retreat behind it as usual. He didn't. "And what did you think of the members of Parliament for Chippenham, Peel and Brooks? Were they pleasant gentlemen?"

He was asking her opinion? "Very committed to their posts, I would say." Was he *genuinely* interested? "And yes, pleasant enough."

"And what sort of age would you estimate them to be?"

Great heaven, he did know how to hold a conversation, after all. But why had he chosen today of all days? And why all the questions about the gentlemen? He wasn't . . . he couldn't possibly be *jealous*, could he?

Hesitantly she replied, "Rather younger than yourself, sir. I think they have only recently begun to realize their ambitions. Mr. Leigh and Mr. Londis were also most knowledgeable and pleasant."

"Hmm."

Tia shot another glance at Mama and was amused to see her eyebrows disappear up into her flounced cap. She was clearly equally astonished by the change in Ansford.

The baron regarded the contents of his teapot again before he picked up the strainer and poured out a pale yellow-green liquid. Tia watched the progress of the cup to his mouth and saw a flicker of distaste as he swallowed the contents down.

"What kind of tea are you drinking, if you don't mind me asking?"

When Ansford's eyes met hers, her stomach tightened.

"St. John's Wort," he replied softly. "Someone recommended it to me." He raised one eyebrow ever so slightly, challenging her, and she had to resist the urge to fan herself rapidly with her napkin.

Odious man. She would never be comfortable in his presence, never. Very well, if he wished to make her feel awkward, she would do the same to him.

She tangled a curl of hair around her finger. "Sir, I was thinking it would be good for Polly to have some diversion. I understand there is to be a fair at Chippenham at the end of July and I would like to take her."

Ansford's fork froze halfway to his mouth. He lowered it slowly and placed it deliberately back on his plate. "A fair? Certainly not."

"But it would be a good incentive to her to study. It's impressive how hard a child will work if promised a treat at the end of it."

"Doubtless you understand more of children than I do, having taught them in the poorhouse," was the lackluster response, "but I must remind you we're a family in mourning."

"I know. But I thought perhaps—"

"You're mistaken. It's a pity, for I hoped we had come to an understanding after our, um, *discussion* the other day."

Tia was aware of her mother sitting up straighter, fascinated by this exchange. She'd told Mama nothing of her altercation with Ansford, not wanting her to know how close she'd come to making an enemy of their benefactor.

She lowered her voice and averted her eyes. "We have, sir. But would you at least give the idea your consideration? The event is nearly a month away."

"Good God, what's digging needles into my leg?" Ansford jumped up in alarm as a small, dark object propelled itself from his lap to the ham on his plate. With impressive speed, he seized the silver cover from the sideboard and clamped it down on top of Polly's kitten, which mewed its resentment.

"What," he inquired in icy tones, "is this?"

Seeing his furious face but also aware of the sounds of feline eating coming from beneath the cover, hysteria threatened. "I fear it is Polly's kitten," she gasped.

An aristocratic eyebrow arched upward. "Indeed? Aldergate!"

At the footman's almost immediate appearance, Tia's amusement was doused by a wash of fear. What did the furious aristocrat plan to do with Polly's pet?

Ansford handed both plate and cover to the bemused servant. "There is a live animal beneath here. Deal with it, if you please."

Tia watched in horror as the hapless creature was whisked out of the breakfast room. She turned anxiously to Ansford, who was glowering at the unwelcome interruption to his breakfast.

She couldn't bear it. "You won't kill it? Please, my lord, don't. It has given Polly such pleasure."

The look he turned on her froze her to the marrow. With the briefest of nods, he turned his back on both her and Mama and stalked out of the room.

A lofty silence descended. Eventually, Mama exclaimed, "Well, I never!"

"I thought he was improving. But I was wrong—the baron's as hardhearted and rude as ever." Tia's temper rose.

Mama shot her a worried look. "What do you think he'll do?"

"I'd like to say he'll eventually see the humor in the situation, but I fear Ansford would choke and suffocate if he attempted to laugh, he's so unused to it. He'll probably have the kitten drowned."

"Oh no, you don't think so? Polly will be devastated."

Of course, she would. Tia would be, too. "I don't believe Lord Ansford understands about tender feelings." She heaved a heartfelt sigh. "His own died with his wife."

"I hope you're mistaken, but he seemed excessively angry with us. Do you think he's a bit peculiar in the head?"

"That wouldn't surprise me at all. Now, I'd best hurry up and see how many French verbs I can get Polly to conjugate before she learns of her kitten's demise. When that news reaches her, we'll have to abandon the curriculum for at least a week."

Unless, of course, she was brave enough to tackle Lord Ansford. Again.

But in his present mood, how could she do so without risking the fate of all those she cared about?

Chapter 15

Hal absently stroked the kitten, curled asleep on his lap. It reminded him of Polly as a baby—once the tiny girl had decided to sleep, nothing short of an earthquake would awaken her.

A pang clutched at his heart, and he pressed a hand against it. Now was not the time to weaken his resolve concerning his daughter, especially with Galatea Wyndham lurking about the place, ready to expose every chink in his emotional armor.

He raised his eyes from the kitten to the window. Outside, the lawns surrounding Foxleaze already showed a brighter green, past midsummer now. Soon his tenant farmers would gather in the hay. As a boy, he'd loved to help with this, and with the wheat harvest. As the young Lord of the Manor and his parents' only child, he was always set triumphantly atop the loaded wagons as they trundled in through the midstrey of the barn.

If it weren't considered unbecoming, Polly could have done this, too—and would doubtless have enjoyed it. Was Galatea correct? Was he being too hard on his daughter?

But if he didn't do something to scotch the speculation surrounding his wife's death, both he and Polly would be pariahs if they ever dared go out in Society again. And if he *did* attempt to quell the gossip by telling the truth, would it improve Polly's lot in any way? Almost certainly not.

He was in a wretched coil. The decisions he'd made to protect his wife's memory and to be sure no scandal ever attached itself to Polly's name had seemed the right ones at the time.

Ought he now to change his mind?

The kitten stirred in his lap and rolled onto its back, stretching and presenting its fluffy tummy. Hal grinned and risked the tiny creature's wrath by tickling it. It reminded him of the time he rescued a litter of kittens from the millpond when he was a boy and had kept—and loved—each and every one.

As this former farm creature was now accorded the status of 'Polly's Kitten,' it needed something to set it apart from its siblings. Perhaps a bow around its neck? Although it would soon lose it. A basket to sleep in maybe, lined with the same color cloth as the ribbon. He would leave the items in the nursery for Polly to find.

Would Galatea be satisfied? It had cut him to the quick that she thought he intended to harm it, forcing him to leave the room lest she see how much she'd offended him.

If he went out of his way to please her, would she think it meant she'd won the battle of wills concerning Polly's schooling? Because he hadn't changed his mind about sending her to the Academy. If Galatea could be relied upon not to let his daughter become as opinionated and willful as herself, there was a chance he might postpone Polly's removal. The pair seemed to like each other, and it would be heartless indeed were he to separate Polly from her new friend so soon.

He gazed out the window once more at the sheen of heat rising from the ground and shimmering across the grass, but all he could see was an image of Galatea, dressed in her finery on the way to dine with the Douglas family. She'd no idea he was watching her, of course, but he couldn't help himself. How jealous he'd been at the thought she would be spending her evening with other gentlemen. Especially looking as ravishing as she did.

Ah, Galatea.

She was so changed since her arrival. Well-fitting clothes direct from the mantua-maker, the services of Paulet and Bessie to assist her with her toilet and the styling of her hair, combined with the fact she was no longer stick-thin, had turned her into a *nonpareil*. The urge to run his eyes appreciatively over every curve of her body and every feature of her face whenever he saw her was becoming harder to resist.

Not that she'd ever let him touch her. She despised him, he was certain. There was nothing about him of which she didn't disapprove or seek to change.

True, there had been the occasional mutual spark when they touched, and he'd known the kindling of desire, but he knew better than to give way to it. Satisfying one's lust with an innocent was anathema.

No. She already held too much sway. As she was antagonistic to everything he believed in, said or did, he was in no hurry to let her augment her power.

It was too damn hot in the house. But he couldn't throw off his clothes and dive into the river as he was wont to do, as he couldn't trust Galatea to stay away from any place he'd ordered her to avoid. He'd have to wait until nightfall now.

Suddenly remembering the fresh tisane of St. John's Wort he'd poured earlier, he lifted the cup and swigged back the tepid liquid. *Ugh.* There had to be a way to make the stuff taste better.

His eye fell on the port decanter, slightly dusty from lack of use, but the liquid inside retained its ruby hue. When he removed the stopper, it smelled good too. Without bothering to hunt for a glass, he tipped the decanter to his lips and relished the buoying warmth sliding down his throat. The taste of the herbal tea was utterly defeated.

"Ah, port. I'd forgotten what a splendid tipple you were." Sighing, he shot his wife's portrait an apologetic look.

"Forgive me, Mary. I swore I'd never touch a drop after you died. But I'm thinking maybe three years is long enough. I'll go to the folly forthwith, to make it up to you."

Having made this resolution, he tucked the kitten into his pocket, seized the decanter, and set off to give his instructions to Aldergate.

Chapter 16

Tia lay on her bed, gazing at the shadowy ceiling, her thoughts prodding her awake, taxing her with the conundrum of Lord Ansford. He was so grim all the time and yet he knew how to be generous and kind. Polly's doll had arrived later the same afternoon, and the child was entranced by it. It might mean less than a hug from her father, but it was a good distraction.

The kitten had been found safe and well in the nursery in its own basket, so Polly still had something to love and to be loved by.

Tia threw off her coverlet. It was so stuffy tonight, even with the window open. A finger of bright moonlight slanted into the room, turning all it touched to a magical silver. Well, if her mind insisted on buzzing around Lord Ansford, she may as well let it. Not that she hoped to draw any conclusions—

The man was such a contradiction.

Of the murder of his wife, she must exonerate him. Any man who put a bow on a kitten was unlikely to have killed his spouse. Nor was he likely to embalm her and secrete the body in the folly, to either gloat over or to remind him of his sin. Tia could no longer imagine the baroness alive in there, imprisoned and insane, hidden from the world so her husband wouldn't have to live with the shame of it.

Yet there was definitely something suspect about the baroness's death, a secret Ansford refused to divulge, a mystery hidden inside the folly. The only way to discover it was by stealth, but how was this to be done? Where did Ansford keep the key? Were there any copies of it?

The housekeeper had a huge ring of keys on a chatelaine, but did she ever leave it unattended? Where did it go when she slept? Did she keep it locked up at night, or beneath her pillow? Did his Lordship's steward, Lynch, have a duplicate set, and how could Tia make inquiries without raising suspicion?

She groaned and sat upright. This was no good, no good at all. She was wide awake now and would think herself into a megrim before morning if she didn't stop. With a sigh, she slipped out of bed, took off her nightgown and pulled on a serviceable cotton walking dress. She was unlikely to meet anyone as she roamed about the house at this hour and anyway, it was too dark for them to tell she wore no underclothes beneath.

Using the moonlight to guide her, Tia slipped out into the passageway and made her way to the main stairwell, with no real idea of where she was going or what she wanted to do.

The cold light cast stark shadows behind the furniture, weapons, and suits of armor adorning the walls of the old entrance hall. She ascended the stairs, her ears alert for every sound, aware of the faces of generations of Pelham ancestors frowning down at her.

Perhaps a perambulation around the old Great Hall would release the nervous energy she'd stored up during the day. She gazed at the terracotta statues of medieval saints and classical philosophers in their shadowy niches and shivered at the touch of their myriad hollow eyes upon her.

Perhaps not. An owl hooted outside, and a bat fluttered past the window. Maybe she would rather be out there with them, with other living creatures instead of in this tomblike, echoing hall.

Despite her swift retreat, she couldn't quite shake the sensation of being watched. The front door stood before her, sturdy with its deep iron nails and heavy latch. It would awaken the entire household if she went out that way. There was nothing for it—she'd have to use the cloister. So long as she didn't encounter the ghosts of its former inhabitants . . .

By the time she emerged onto the lawn beyond the archway, there was moisture on her upper lip. Lord, how easy it was to succumb to one's imaginings. She mustn't allow herself to be afraid of the supernatural—only the corporeal could do one *actual* harm.

Was Ansford in the folly? It was late, past midnight at a guess. No, there were no lamps shining from the tower. She was trying to decide where she might walk without setting all the dogs off when she caught a movement out of the corner of her eye.

A tall figure was striding into the trees in the direction of the river.

Ansford. It had to be him. Wherever was he going at this hour of the night? The only way to answer the question would be to follow him.

Her nerves fizzed with the thrill of being the hunter, stalking its prey. What a heady sense of power it gave one, to be in pursuit of the unwary.

When she reached the belt of trees, however, her quarry was gone. The moonlight barely penetrated the burgeoning foliage, and she had to stand motionless while her eyes adjusted.

If he were still walking through the woods, should she not be able to hear his footsteps crackling amongst the twigs and last year's fallen leaves? Yet she could hear nothing but the thundering of her heart and the rush of blood in her ears. Night descended about her like soft velvet, and when she began to go forward again, she imagined it was pushing gently against her, urging her to go back.

Gradually a new sound became audible, a sound like the wind soughing through branches. The rushing of the river.

She knew the stand of trees opened out before it reached the bank, so the moonlight would be able to penetrate. As she'd lost her quarry, she might as well walk down to the water and enjoy its soothing flow before attempting to go back to the house.

Suddenly she noticed something pale lying crumpled by the water's edge and when she went closer to examine it, it turned out to be a pile of clothes.

Her heart thudded to a halt. Ansford must be here, bathing, as was his wont. He must be some way down the river though, for she couldn't hear any splashing. It would probably be a good idea to remove herself immediately. The baron would be furious if he knew she'd penetrated his private swimming spot. But as she turned to go, she noticed something small glinting on top of the pile of clothing.

A key. Her heart leapt into her throat.

Could this be *the* key? The one to the folly? She'd seen what she thought was a key around Ansford's neck when she'd first set eyes on him, when she'd believed him to be a hermit.

Temptation gnawed at her, mingled with curiosity and guilt. There might never be another opportunity like this one. She could take the key, unlock the folly and replace the key before the baron returned from his swim. As soon as he'd gone off to bed, she'd get a lantern and explore the tower.

She wouldn't touch anything, only look. When Ansford arrived in the morning, he'd merely assume he'd forgotten to lock the door the previous day.

I must know what is in there, for Polly's sake.

Hopefully, there would be absolutely nothing nefarious, and her own mind could find ease. And she might permit herself to like Ansford as much as she wanted to.

Buoyed up by this reasoning, Tia picked up the key with a trembling hand. She'd just turned away to creep back into the shadows when there was a great whoosh of water behind her.

"Stop."

The familiar voice held a tone she dared not disobey.

Chapter 17

Slowly she turned around. Lord Ansford was advancing toward her up the bank, the water streaming from his muscular body, his hair hanging in dark tendrils against his shoulders, like Poseidon emerging from the waves. Or Heracles maybe, considering the powerful planes of his chest and the fascinating bunches of muscle spanning his flat stomach.

Tia backed away, but he continued his advance. She couldn't help herself—her gaze raked up and down his superbly sculpted form, taking in every single inch of him. It was too dark to see the expression in his eyes—they were mere shadows beneath the black slashes of eyebrows—but his mouth was set in a grim line.

He didn't stop to clothe himself but came on relentlessly, menace in every step.

She'd seen him angry before, but this was different. She continued to back away until she fetched up short against some obstacle and could go no further. Her hands pressed against the rough bark of an oak tree as she flattened herself against its trunk, wordlessly waiting for the sea god's wrath to fall.

As he came closer, she forced her eyes upward and resolutely kept them there, despite the temptation to admire and wonder at his body as long as possible.

When he was so close she could barely focus on him, he stopped, leaned in, and placed a hand on either side of her head against the tree.

The glitter of his eyes made her pulse skip. Her knees had turned to jelly, and only her awkward grip on the tree held her up. The beat of her heart was so rapid she half expected it to fly right out of her chest, like a frightened bird.

Holding up the key in shaking fingers, she breathed, "I'm sorry, I didn't mean any harm, my lord. Take it back, please."

"I don't need it. Not yet. And it seems rather formal to call me 'my lord' when you have me completely naked before you, stripped of all vestige of rank and power."

She licked her lips. "I wouldn't exactly say that."

"You should call me Henry, Galatea. The time for formality between us has most definitely passed."

Not only her knees, but her legs had lost the ability to hold her upright. At this rate, she was going to end up slithering down the tree like a worm. But not from fear.

The realization hit her with the force of a hurricane. She desired him, wanted him, more than she'd wanted anything in her life before. In her heart, she knew it had happened when first she'd laid eyes on him, but she'd buried it deeply to protect herself.

Or to fool herself.

Now the need awoke with overwhelming violence. Her mouth went dry, and she couldn't help wondering what she would experience if she ran her hands along those silvered flanks.

"You should definitely get dressed, or you'll catch a chill," she urged. No, *pleaded*. This temptation was absolute torture.

"As will you," he replied softly, "if you go about without your underthings on."

How could he possibly know? She glanced down and flushed.

Freed from their usual constrictions, her nipples stood

out hard and proud, pushing against the thin fabric of her walking dress. Damn the man for noticing. *Damn him.*

He came closer until there was barely a whisper of decency between their bodies, and shifted a hand to touch a lock of her hair. A light tug, and the curl sprang back and bounced against her neck. His eyes followed it, then examined her heated face.

"I wondered what you looked like with your hair down. It's like a dark cloud cloaking your shoulders, framing your face."

"Very poetic, my lord." Why did she sound so breathless?

"Henry. Or Hal if you prefer. My friends, when I had some, used to call me Hal."

What was going on here? Was he angry, or not? She offered him the key again but he simply shook his head and gave her a mirthless grimace.

"No. I haven't finished with you yet."

She was most definitely in danger. Bravely holding his gaze, she moistened her lips. "Do you mean to punish me?"

"Perhaps. It depends upon your answer to my question. What cause have I given you to think I'd have my daughter's kitten drowned?"

"I . . . I . . ." She couldn't think straight. His breath on her face smelled sweet, like the best port wine. A drop of water from his hair splashed onto her neck and trickled down inside the front of her walking dress. He watched its progress before brushing his knuckles across the silvery trail, igniting a line of fire across her bosom. Her nipples ached from straining against the cloth that confined them.

Softly he repeated his question, and added, "Do you truly think me so inhuman? Can you not trust me?"

She swallowed hard. "How can I trust you when you won't tell me what's in the folly?"

"Because it doesn't affect you. It's private and will remain so. There's nothing terrible there, believe me."

"Hal—"

"Shh." He placed a cool finger across her lips. They suddenly became as sensitive as her nipples, and she squirmed against the tree, aching for she knew not what. Helplessly, she gazed up at the man before her, the moonlight blazing on his bare shoulders.

What an amazing mouth he had. A slender upper lip, a full lower lip with a bow-shaped curve between and the slightest of upward quirks at the corners. How much would she give right now to hear words of tenderness issue from those devilishly tempting lips?

His finger stroked along her mouth and under her lower lip, then dropped to create a gentle pressure beneath her chin.

"Would you consider me a monster if I kissed you?"

"W—Why would you want to?"

"At this particular point in time," he drawled, "I can't think of any reason not to."

She closed her eyes as his delectable mouth brushed across hers. Like the touch of a flame, it ignited answering fires throughout her body. His damp hair trailed coolly along her cheek, and further drips found their way into the warm cleft between her breasts.

His mouth widened against her own and she pulled back to stare at him. Yes, incredibly, Lord Ansford was happy. And what a devastating smile he had. It knocked all the air out of her.

"You . . . you should smile more often."

"I haven't had much reason to, before now." His deep, intriguing voice washed over her like a benediction as pleasure swelled within her.

"And you should come out more often with your hair down and no underclothes on," he added.

There was a faint clink. Her nervous fingers had dropped the key. She made no attempt to retrieve it. Nor did he.

He reached out to the ties closing the flap at the front of her dress. She was completely in his thrall now, unable to do anything to restrain him as he tugged at the bow and smoothed the cloth back from her breasts.

Intent on what he was doing, Tia no longer clung to the tree. Instead, her hands were glued to the silken skin on his back, her fingers digging into the firm flesh, pulling his body closer. Her breasts were now bared to his view and his warm, knowing hands. One palm cupped her tender flesh and stroked it admiringly. She heard his breath catch in his throat as his other smoothed across the taut nipple, brushing its peak with his thumb.

Hot desire gushed into her belly, between her legs, in all her deepest, most intimate places. *Oh Lord, oh Lord.* This should not be happening. He was her benefactor, her superior, a dangerous, unpredictable man. There was no need to put herself even more into his power than she was already. And if this caress were to lead to anything more, what effect might it have on her future, her mother's future?

No, it wasn't worth the risk. Lust was shallow and quickly sated, she'd heard. Succumbing to it was too high a price to pay.

She was summoning her scattered wits to put a stop to the caress when Hal suddenly pulled away, swearing softly.

"What the deuce am I doing? Galatea, cover yourself, I beg you. Forgive me. I'm a fool and a brute—I'm so sorry. I swear on my worthless life I'll never take advantage of you again." He swung away from her and strode back to the pile of his clothes.

She collapsed against the tree like a deflated balloon. As her shaking fingers struggled with the ties of her dress, she sought to congratulate herself on a fortunate escape. But her body, throbbing with unfulfilled need, told her quite the opposite.

Moments later he returned, no longer a moon-etched god of the night, but an awkward and angry English aristocrat in a damp shirt.

"The key, if you please."

She bent and fumbled about among the old acorns and leaf mold until her hand touched metal. As she handed it to him, his fingers brushed hers, and she experienced again the heady leap of desire. But he had already retreated from her, back into his melancholy isolation.

He hung the cord around his neck and gathered up his jacket. "I'll walk you back to the house. I know my way through these woods far better than you."

Eager now to be away from the man who'd exerted such devastating power, she kept her distance. Only when they reached the shadow of the archway did she break the loaded silence.

"My lord . . . Hal. I'm sorry I've mistrusted you. I hope you can forgive me for being such a nuisance. You have my promise I won't pry into your affairs, or your past, any further. I'll keep away from the folly, and the library, and the cloisters and—"

He turned and caught her gently by the elbow. "Galatea, I appreciate that promise. I insist on the folly alone being sacrosanct. Your presence in the rest of the abbey I find I can bear very well. In return, I ask only that you forget tonight and carry on exactly as you always did. Agreed?"

She peeped at him from beneath lowered lashes. Truly, he was the most handsome man she'd ever seen, particularly when his face was soft and earnest like this, mellowed by the darkness. She nodded slowly as he held the cloister door open for her to enter.

"I will," she agreed.

But she knew it was a lie.

Chapter 18

Hal smote his fists on his desk, making the inkwells jump. This was the third time he'd attempted to check Lynch's figures—and the third time he'd come up with a different total. Very well, if he wasn't in the right state of mind for figures, he'd write the long overdue letter to his aunt, Dorothea. They'd barely exchanged a word since Mary's death, but he knew Dorothea adored children and would love to know how Polly was getting on.

Reaching for a quill, he discovered it was blunt and started whittling it irritably with a pocketknife. His first attempt was a failure and all he achieved was blots. His second attempt was even worse, so he gave up in disgust and marched across to the window.

Flinging it open, he gazed out at yet another beautiful day, the first of July, the weather sultry and hot, the air filled with the lazy buzzing of bees and the distant cooing of doves. He wondered if Polly and Galatea would be outside enjoying themselves.

Galatea. *Tia*. His stomach tightened as he tried to thrust away the unwelcome memories of yesterday evening. What in heaven had he been thinking? He had no right to kiss her, to maul her in such a debauched way. Deuce take it, he'd never treated any woman in so ungentlemanly a fashion. Had he become a barbarian since his retreat from Society?

He chewed on an inky forefinger but barely noticed the bitter taste. Why was he letting himself care what Tia thought of him? By now, he should be indifferent to the opinions of others.

It wasn't as if he'd set out to make an impression on the woman. Quite the opposite in fact, but now he found he couldn't bear to have her thinking badly of him. Any normal fellow would find ways of making amends, but he'd removed himself so far from normality, he had no idea how to proceed.

Cursing himself for his cowardice, he'd deliberately avoided going down for breakfast this morning, knowing how uncomfortable the atmosphere would be. He would surely have betrayed himself with a look, a gesture, or the tone of his voice. Until he'd plotted out how to gain Tia's forgiveness, it was best to avoid her.

Turning away from the window, he stared up at Mary's portrait. These last three years, he'd continued to converse with her shade, asking it, too, for forgiveness. Now, there was no vestige of her left, except what he could see in the face and demeanor of Polly. Did his self-sacrifice, his punishing regimen, the monument he was building to Mary's memory, serve anyone but himself?

And was he *really* doing the right thing for Polly by hardening her heart?

The blue-gray eyes in the painting stared back at him, bright and lively, as Mary had been in life. He waited for the familiar pang of distress, and when it didn't come fast enough, forced himself to remember her as he'd last seen her, lying bleeding and broken at the foot of the folly tower. Closing his eyes, he reminded himself of the huge wash of guilt he'd experienced as he made that last, most painful farewell.

A soft tap on the door roused him from his reverie. His breath caught when he opened it to find Tia standing in the passageway, twisting her hands together in agitation. Steeling himself to show nothing but regret, he stood aside and ushered her in.

She walked across to his desk and pressed her palms flat on the top. Closing the door, he stood with his back against it and waited for her to speak. It wouldn't do, venturing too close, not knowing how far he could trust his self-control.

"You didn't come down to breakfast." She kept her face averted as she spoke.

"No. You must know why."

"You didn't wish to see me. You didn't want to remember what happened last night." Was there a wobble in her voice?

"You're wrong there, Tia. I don't think I'll ever forget what I did last night. I can't forgive myself for behaving like a callow youth."

She spun to face him, a charmingly rosy flush staining her cheeks. "Callow youth?"

"Precisely. No matter how much I might have wished to touch you, that was *not* the way to go about it."

She narrowed her eyes at him. "So how *should* you have gone about it, Hal?"

Was she teasing him? "Can't we let the subject drop? I asked for your forgiveness last night, and I beg for it even more humbly now. You have my permission to avoid me if you wish. I won't blame you for it. If you want to slap my face, or stamp on my toe, perhaps empty a jug of water on top of me, please do so. I fully deserve whatever punishment you can derive."

She raised an eyebrow at this. "I never thought to hear such humility from you. Believe me, I don't expect you to do penance for a misguided action. However, I *am* thinking of blackmailing you with your indiscretion."

He hadn't expected that. His mouth twitched. "Out with it. What must I do?" He banished the grin. Ashamed he might be, but she mustn't think him soft.

"I want you to let me take Polly to the fair. Mama doesn't wish to go—she has an invitation with Mrs. Brooks she'd like to honor."

"You don't want to go to the Brooks' too?" Secretly, he was pleased she hadn't made mixing with the local gentry her priority.

"No. Polly has behaved herself impeccably, and as I mentioned before, has earned her reward. You'd be proud of her. Please say we can go. I'll see she comes to no harm."

"If your mama's not going, who'll chaperone you?"

The blush on her cheeks spread farther, heating her neck and—he was ashamed to notice—her breast. He grazed his fist against the stone of the door frame, needing the distraction of pain.

"I wondered if perhaps *you* would accompany us. The fair is on the twenty-second of this month."

"Me?" He was flabbergasted. She wanted his company? *Impossible*.

"Indeed. It has to be yourself, or else a servant. I wasn't sure you'd want us to go to Chippenham with only a servant. I need someone who can drive your Stanhope gig."

"I'm certain I can spare Aldergate."

She regarded him levelly for a moment with those melting brown eyes of hers. "For Polly's sake, Hal, I think it had far better be you."

"Galatea, please. How can I show myself in such a public place when I've lived here so quietly for so long? I'd find it intolerable."

"You were once much used to being seen and heard in public. A country fair is nothing compared to the noisy chambers of Westminster or the glittering ballrooms of Carlton House. Or so I imagine. At the beginning of this conversation, you agreed to do whatever I asked."

Silence drew out between them while she held his gaze expectantly. An unwelcome sensation, of being about to lose a battle, swamped him. "Very well, I'll come to the fair. At least I have some time to prepare myself mentally."

Her dark-lashed eyes still traversed his face, and her delightful rosebud mouth was solemn.

He rolled his eyes. "There's something else, isn't there?"

"I'm afraid so. I . . . um . . . I think we would attract less notice in Chippenham were you not dressed entirely in black. Perhaps a colored waistcoat for the occasion?"

Hal blinked. "A colored waistcoat? Tia, you ask too much."

"And a blue superfine jacket instead of your black one?"

His mouth tightened. "If you're ashamed to be seen with me, why ask me at all?"

"For Polly's sake, as I told you. If you won't change your apparel, can I at least cut your hair? I believe I've done a tolerable job with hers."

"Symons always trims my hair."

"Yes, but I wager he's never had to cut it when it was so long before."

Was there no winning an argument with the chit? He was beginning to think he ought to go back to avoiding or ignoring her.

There remained the option of sending her away.

Something close to panic sprang to life in the pit of his stomach and goosebumps broke out on his skin. Could he do that now? Could he *really* send her and her mother away?

"All right. You may cut my hair. Best do it now before I change my mind."

"Now?" The blush seemed to have spread even farther. Exactly how far down her lovely breast had it progressed?

Running a finger around inside his cravat, he pondered his body's reaction. He'd been chilled a moment ago, but now the room was unpleasantly hot.

Tia hesitated. Maybe she hadn't expected so speedy a capitulation. She was nervous of him, anxious to get too close—not without good reason—and had perhaps hoped for time to build herself up to the moment. He'd stolen that time away from her and was fascinated to see if she would renege.

But Miss Galatea Wyndham was made of stern stuff. "Very well. I'll fetch an apron."

"And I shall ring for warm water to be brought up to my chamber," he offered. He held the door open for her as she left, and paused there a moment, watching her trot down the stairs, wondering if she had any idea at all how momentous a decision this was for him.

He sincerely hoped that, unlike Samson, the shearing of his locks wouldn't render him as weak as a child. For he was going to need all his strength to resist the allure of Miss Galatea Wyndham.

Chapter 19

With her new striped dress protected by a pinned apron, and fully armed with her sharpest sewing scissors, Tia arrived at Hal's suite some ten minutes later.

The baron had replaced his outer clothing with a thin silk dressing gown, beneath which his shirt flopped open at the neck. A white towel hung about his shoulders, a second one within reach beside the porcelain basin.

She sucked in a breath and took a tighter hold on her scissors. The valet was absent.

Hal's blue eyes met hers. "I sincerely hope I can trust you, Tia."

"That remains to be seen," she teased. "Now wet your hair for me, please."

He sat forward and obligingly dunked his head in the basin, then reached blindly for a jug so he could pour more water over his head.

When he came up again, his hair clung to his face and neck in a way that reminded her vividly of how he'd looked the previous night, naked and dripping in the moonlight. A shiver of desire sang through her body. Hurriedly she thrust a towel onto his head and began kneading to take some of the dampness out, making sure he couldn't see her expression.

When she'd regained control of her errant imagination, she draped the towel across his shoulders and took a fortifying breath.

What had she been thinking of when she offered to cut his hair? It meant she'd have to touch him, bend her head close to his, hear the sound of his breathing and smell the compelling musky scent of his body. How was she to keep her own reactions under control and wield a pair of scissors at the same time? If she couldn't calm her response to him, he was going to end up an absolute fright.

She sensed him observing her and steeled her features to a businesslike demeanor. "First I must take out the tangles." She jabbed a tortoiseshell comb into his hair. It caught in the knotted ends, and he winced.

"Bother. I'll have to do it with my fingers."

"I shall endeavor to be brave," he promised.

She worked her way around him, striving to keep her distance, teasing out the knots between her fingers until she was able to apply the comb without resistance. Such thick, heavy hair. It sprang up from a widow's peak and a central parting to frame his superbly sculpted face. But his locks were definitely too long.

As she reached for the scissors and began to cut, she sensed his gaze on her face in the mirror, like a physical caress.

"Why are you staring at my reflection?"

"Sorry. Am I putting you off?"

He most certainly was. "Yes." She *tutted* in annoyance. Struggling to retain her composure, she circled to the front of him to tease some of his hair forward. It flopped into his eyes, causing him to close them, but this did nothing for her equanimity, as she was forced to brace her legs against his knees as she leaned toward him.

Damnation. Now she couldn't get the vision of his moon-silvered, naked body out of her mind. It was as if someone had etched it onto the inside of her eyelids and it was all she saw, whenever she closed them. Or blinked.

Concentrate, Tia. Concentrate. She had a lethal weapon in her hands and, if she failed to wield it correctly, it would leave the eighth Baron Ansford looking worse than before she started.

Carefully, she thinned out the hair at the front, bringing it forward to brush his forehead, just enough to soften the hairline and partially conceal the worry lines that gave character to his brow.

Curse it. Now she had to fight the urge to run her fingers along the creases, smooth them out, rub away the furrow between the brows and stroke the soft skin at his temples.

She bit sharply on her lower lip to bring herself back to her senses. Best get the front part dealt with quickly, before attending to the back and sides. It was too easy to be distracted by the play of light and shadow on the man's face, the strong cheekbones, the mobile mouth with its full, eminently kissable, lower lip.

What if she were to reach out a finger and trace the tantalizing crease between his lips? Or lean forward and brush her own against them? Would he once again become an elemental creature of the night, taking charge of her body, binding her soul?

For now, he was under her control, tamed, obliging. But she sensed the veneer of respectability was thin. He'd need little invitation to reach for her again, caress her breasts with his warm, knowing hands, and drag her hard against his body.

"Ouch!" The blue eyes flashed open.

"I'm so sorry. Let me see. No, I haven't drawn blood— it's only a scratch. I need to change my position." Tongue clamped between her teeth, Tia shifted around, cutting and snipping as speedily as she dared, more aware than ever this haircutting was an *extremely* bad idea.

Soon the towel was covered with damp curls, and part of the back of Hal's neck was revealed, as were his ears. Although the hair was wet and not yet properly arranged into the 'Windswept' style she was hoping for, she could see the transformation already. If only he would do away with that lowering expression of his, he could be quite the buck and would have the ladies falling at his feet.

Ha, what ladies?

If he wouldn't go out or invite anyone to visit, he would continue to rot away here in his loneliness, hiding in his folly.

Only he was no longer alone. He had *her*. She was his friend, and she'd never abandon him, certainly not before she'd returned him to the world. Mama was right. She was making a project of the baron, exactly as she had with Mr. Roach. But her reasons were so very different.

Facing Hal again to ensure the hair at the sides was even, Tia was subjected once more to his penetrating scrutiny. He couldn't take his eyes off her today, it seemed. She mustn't give him any reason to berate her.

Avoiding the lure of his gaze, she lowered her eyes—and spotted the key hung around his neck.

Her heart sank. How could she be a true friend to him when this secret lay like a chasm between them? She had every hope now of being able to change his mind about Polly—all she needed to do was to teach the girl how to deal with taunts and bullies. That could be done without turning Polly into a heartless, wooden puppet.

But the issue of the folly, and the mysterious circumstances of the late Lady Ansford's fall continued to goad her.

Shaking away the thought, she dug her hands into the hair on either side of his face and pushed it back, searching for any unevenness. His breath hitched at her touch, but she forced herself to do it again and peered closely at her handiwork. Now the hair was drying and had been relieved of so much weight, it had developed a pleasing wave.

Hal raised his head slightly to look at her, and she retreated a pace to admire the overall effect.

Her knees trembled.

God, he was beautiful. And he gazed at her as if she might be the most wonderful thing he'd ever seen. But with her stupid apron, stray locks of her hair hanging down, and a good quantity of his own shorn hair adhering to her, he couldn't *possibly* be admiring her. She must be reading it wrong.

"Tia."

She backed away quickly, unpinned her apron, and shook it out before brushing at her dress. "Stand up, please."

He had to stop looking at her like that. It made her want to throw herself into his arms. Grabbing a clothes brush from his dressing table, she cleared the stray hairs from his shoulders.

His broad, powerful shoulders.

The floor was now covered in hair. A servant could clean it up later. She needed to get out of this room.

"Tia."

She avoided his eyes. "I must be getting back. They'll be wondering where I've got to."

"Wait. Don't you want to know what I think of your handiwork?"

He peeled off his dressing gown and shook it off, then threw it over a screen before bending to admire himself in the mirror. She hovered behind him, staring at his reflection, and met his eyes in the glass. He straightened and turned to face her. His pupils were huge, almost eclipsing the blue.

"Capital job, capital. Do you think I pass muster now?"

Staring up at him, her gaze snagged on his firm, masculine mouth. He smiled at her, a rare, devastating glory, like the sun coming out from behind a cloud.

She forgot to breathe. *Oh Lord.*

Slowly, daringly, she stretched out her palm to caress his cheek. Immediately he pressed his hand atop hers and closed his eyes.

There was no denying the message that passed between their bodies. When Hal opened his eyes again, the heat she saw in them was like an open fire on a winter's day, hot, inviting.

Ravenous.

It came as no surprise to Tia that a kiss should follow such a feral, triumphant grin. And what a kiss. Hard, possessive, hungry.

The pulse of desire she'd felt that night by the river flooded back, her body taut with a hunger of its own. But how to assuage it?

His lips pressed against hers, massaging and manipulating them, and she felt her own blossom beneath the pressure, increasing the delectable sensation.

What would happen if she kissed him back?

He pulled away for a moment, and she gazed at his sumptuous mouth, aching to feel it again. Instinct took over, and she tugged his head down, tracing the intriguing contours of his mouth with her tongue. This elicited a low growl from him, and instantly she was held fast as his tongue invaded her mouth, penetrating her with masculine potency.

As their kiss deepened, her mind reeled. Would he notice, would he mind, if she touched him?

She lowered one hand, sliding it tentatively down his side, relishing the firm flesh beneath the crisp linen of his shirt. Her throat went dry at the thought of what it might be like to palm his skin beneath the shirt, to examine all the places a woman's hands were not supposed to go, except in the arms of her lover.

A lover? Tia broke the kiss abruptly, pushing out of Hal's embrace. Her lips burned for him, her body ached for him, but was she prepared to take him as a lover? For surely this was what, by welcoming his kiss, she was inviting him to become.

She'd no idea where such a situation might end, but there was too high a risk of it not working out in her favor. So many young women had fallen foul of the wiles of men. In the poorhouse such women, and their bastard children, were legion.

Did she genuinely believe Hal the kind of man to take a woman's virginity without the benefit of marriage?

Afraid to ask herself, Tia seized her scissors, muttered, "I'm sorry," and stumbled out of the room, cheeks burning.

Chapter 20

The baron hadn't joined Tia and Mama for luncheon, nor for dinner later the same day. This had been an enormous relief to Tia, convinced she'd thrown herself at him like a complete wanton, no better than the meanest doxy in Selbury.

An uncomfortable night had been spent fretting about her terrible lapse of self-control, partly because she didn't know how she could live with herself. Mostly because she didn't know how she could live with Hal either, certainly not without wanting to progress what had started between them.

She bolted down her breakfast in hopes of being finished before he came down, needing time to ascertain what on earth she was going to do.

"I saw the baron yesterday evening," Mama remarked casually, glancing up from a letter she'd been reading. "He'd had his hair cut and appeared most presentable."

Tia's cup rattled back onto its saucer, splashing tea on her hand.

"What is it?" Mama put down the letter and eyed her closely.

Tia grabbed a napkin to mop up the spill. "Nothing at all. The cup slipped."

"Tell me. I always know when you're hiding something."

I very much hope you don't. But cutting Ansford's hair was a minor misdemeanor compared with her other sins. "*I* cut it, Mama," she confessed.

"*You*?"

"You must admit it needed cutting."

"I can't argue there. But it was outrageously improper, Galatea. How could you not know?"

"Nothing happened." Tia hoped the heat flooding her cheeks would be put down to the warm day, and the hot cup of tea.

"Not in front of his valet. Who *was* present, I assume? But it doesn't make your behavior any more acceptable."

Tia had to pray Mama didn't think to question Symons about the incident. "Ansford's not *that* sort of man anyway." Although she'd proved herself to be *that* sort of lady.

"One can never tell with a dark horse like Lord Ansford," came the crisp reply. "I find him impossible to read. Don't you?"

"I think I may be growing accustomed to his ways."

Her mother eyed her keenly. "Good. But don't ever let the man take advantage of your innocence, child. If it seems he's interested in you in the wrong sort of way, if he makes you at all uncomfortable, we'll simply save up the allowance he gives us and leave. We're part of Society again, no longer alone and friendless. Why, I have received another invitation from Lady Douglas only this morning."

Tia was no longer listening. Go? Leave Foxleaze?

Leave Hal?

Her stomach contracted painfully. "There's no need to leave, is there? Besides, if Ansford were to develop a *tendre* for me, would you really object? Aren't all mothers keen to see their daughters wed—"

"Good morning, Mrs. Wyndham, Miss Wyndham. I trust I find you well this morning?"

Hal.

The atmosphere hummed like a bowstring. After mumbling a response, Mama hid herself behind her letter while Tia dabbed her napkin at an invisible spot on the tablecloth.

How much had he heard? Wretched man. Why couldn't he make a noise when he approached, like any thoughtful person?

There was an awkward silence while Hal's chair was drawn up for him and his paper set by his elbow. Tia finally dared raise her eyes, fearing to see a knowing look on his face. If he thought for one moment she wanted, nay, *expected*, him to offer for her, she would die of shame.

Her heart gave a lurch when she saw him.

The haircut had truly transformed him from ascetic hermit to resplendent Adonis, perfect in form and feature, bright-eyed, intelligent, and devilishly attractive. He'd shaved, dressed with care—albeit in his habitual black—and observed his companions with interest rather than indifference, with pleasure rather than anger.

He looked, in fact, very nearly . . . normal. If anyone so devastatingly handsome could be called such.

"You must think me rude, reading my paper at table." His tone was easy, relaxed.

"Oh, not at all," Mama replied, "so long as you don't object to me perusing my correspondence."

"Not in the least."

Tia watched this exchange, inwardly congratulating her mother on appearing so poised in light of what Hal might—or might not—have overheard.

The small teapot was brought in. He was still trying the St. John's Wort, even though it must taste foul. He genuinely *was* taking some of her suggestions to heart.

Triumph upon triumph!

If only it weren't for that damned folly, and his blind refusal to accept what was best for his daughter, she could almost . . . she could almost *like* the man.

"I trust the room is feline-free at present? I've had two pairs of breeches ruined already by the mountaineering monster."

"I believe so, sir." Tia was thankful to have her thoughts steered in another direction. "One might imagine the kitten has taken to you."

"Indeed. I have the scratches to prove it." He gazed at her intently. "Not because I've been unkind to it, you realize. It simply plays a trifle too . . . enthusiastically."

She acknowledged the hit with a brief nod and waited to see if he was prepared to make any further attempt at 'normal' conversation.

His long fingers caressed the curved sides of the small teapot, making her recall with a shock how those same fingers had caressed her naked breast that mad midsummer's night. Damn the man. Was he doing it on purpose?

"Is your preserve not to your liking, Miss Wyndham?"

What preserve? Oh, her breakfast, or what remained of it. Forgotten, apparently.

"I'm not as hungry as I thought, my lord."

Her mother folded up her letter and placed it beside her plate. "Are you content to have us call you by your title, sir? It seems rather formal at the breakfast table."

"Quite right," he agreed affably. "We are family after all. I'm happy to be Henry, or Hal, whatever you prefer."

Family? This was a development of enormous significance. Tia had never heard him use the word 'family' before. Surely this augured well for her plans for Polly?

The next moment, he spoiled it all by saying, "Although I believe I should call Galatea 'Miss Wyndham' in front of Polly. The child needs to respect her elders and betters, at least while Tia remains her teacher."

At least while Tia remains her teacher . . . What on earth did he mean?

That he intended to send Polly off to the dreaded Academy earlier than planned? Or that Tia might soon be connected with Polly in a different capacity entirely?

If only she hadn't made that comment about marriage. She was going to have to have a private word with Hal. He needed to explain his cryptic remark.

An explanation she needed, and *soon*.

Chapter 21

It was proving harder to be in close proximity to Tia than Hal had imagined. Every time he saw her, his thoughts darted up inappropriate avenues, recalling her soft breasts in his palms, the silk of her rose-petal lips as they surrendered their honeyed secrets. The vivid imaginings which laid siege to his brain were wholly unsuited to the breakfast table, and most definitely *not* the kind of thing one should be thinking about in the presence of a young lady's mother.

Thus, it was with great trepidation that he allowed Tia to lead him into the Great Hall as soon as their meal was done. He wasn't afraid of her, of course—only of his own ability to keep her at arms' length. She was meant to be under his protection, for heaven's sake. What kind of a rake would he be if he were to despoil an innocent under his own roof? Mary's shade would most certainly not approve.

As he closed the door behind him, it struck him with full force he hadn't worked in the folly yesterday, probably the first time in years he'd missed a day. Mary's restless spirit wouldn't approve of *that* either.

He gave Tia his full attention. "So, what did you want to inquire about that was best dealt with in private? You will have aroused your mama's suspicions, you know. She's nobody's fool."

Tia's eyes scanned his face. He raised an eyebrow. Was there something wanting in his appearance? He'd done his best to live up to her expectations today—at least her expectations concerning his outward appearance.

"Is there . . . is there something you have planned I don't know about?" Her voice sounded unusually tight, even hesitant.

"What do you mean?"

"I mean, have you made any particular decisions concerning Polly's future? Or . . . or mine?"

He smiled. Was she insecure? "Why no, I haven't changed my mind about anything, if that's what you mean."

"Oh." She frowned.

He was missing something, wasn't he? If he hadn't shut himself off from the rest of the world these last three years, he might have been better at working out what it was. "Please tell me what's bothering you. I'm no good at nuance."

She chewed on her lip, and he clenched his jaw. What was to stop him sweeping her into his arms and kissing the abused flesh, or abusing it himself with all the force of his pent-up passion?

They needed to get this conversation done with quickly before he made a fool of himself.

Again.

Tia tilted her chin. "I only wanted to remind you we are taking Polly to the fair at Chippenham later this month."

Deuce take it—he'd forgotten. He was nowhere near ready to go out in public. Especially not with Tia and Polly, when he was finding it such a struggle to keep the lid on his desires.

"I've considered it further and find I have deep reservations." Hal wouldn't go into the reasons why. That would be putting too much power into those small, female hands.

"I know you think it too frivolous when this is meant to be a house of mourning," she countered. "But Polly is ready to move on, even if you are not. You may deny yourself pleasure if you wish, but there's no need to starve her of enjoyment."

They were back to that argument, were they? Perhaps it was just as well. "You've been in this household barely six weeks, yet you presume to know the innermost thoughts and needs of its occupants."

"I don't mean to belittle your feelings." Tia came closer. "Your devotion to your wife's memory does you credit. But anyone will tell you it's excessive, especially when imposed on a nine-year-old girl."

Far too close to the bone. "You're certainly free with your opinions, Tia."

"As you pointed out earlier, Hal, we are a family— though distantly related—and families are frank with one another, even when they know their words will hurt."

He rolled his eyes at the terracotta statues in their niches. "Now I remember why I chose to stop speaking to people. So my words couldn't be used against me. All the same, my mind is made up. Polly is *not* going to the fair."

Tia's expression was no longer earnest. A spark of flinty anger lurked in the depths of those melting brown eyes. "Surely the baroness would have wanted her to go about and enjoy herself? You keep the poor child locked up like a caged bird, and it does neither of you any good."

He went cold and gave an involuntary shudder. "That was what Mary used to say." The memory was all too painfully clear. "She said I was so bound up in my ideals, and my political machinations, I'd forgotten how to enjoy life. We didn't go out enough, we didn't travel, I was always working and she felt caged . . . Don't women perceive such pleasures have to be earned and are thus all the sweeter in moderation?"

Tia frowned. "Didn't she go on visits, or into town for the shops and the markets?"

"Oh, she did all those things—don't mistake me. But I expected her to do them alone when I was busy. I could see no harm." Why were they talking about Mary now? Weren't they meant to be discussing Polly?

"You must have been busy all the time, for your wife to have made such a complaint."

"I was, and I know it. But I was a man driven. Who wouldn't be, with the sufferings of the slaves, the lace and blanket makers, the wounded veterans and the starving populace? I worked feverishly to bring about governmental reform—"

Tia laid a hand on his arm with a soft, "I know you did."

He swallowed. Had she any idea what her nearness was doing to him? He wanted *her*, not her pity.

Gently, he extricated himself. "I assumed once I'd achieved my ends, there'd be plenty of time to spend together . . . but it was too late. She didn't tell me . . . she hid from me—"

"What did she hide from you?"

"I've revealed too much," he growled. "I've dropped my guard. I'm sorry, Tia, but this has to stop. You can't keep prying into my affairs or my past, for what you discover would hurt you as much as it hurts me."

She narrowed her eyes. "I wasn't prying," she retorted. "I was seeking an explanation for what seemed to me an irrational decision."

He gave a bitter laugh. "Irrational not to approve Polly's desire to attend the fair? I think I've explained my reasons with perfect logic. What's *really* irrational is the way I've let you get under my skin, divert me from my duty, and tempt me beyond all reason."

"Tempt you? I never meant to."

No, of course, she hadn't. The fault was all his. But if he were to move past this growing obsession with her, he would need *her* to exercise restraint as well.

He took her by the shoulders and brought his face close to hers. "My dear," he ground out, "you'd shrivel up in shame if you could see the visions running through my mind right now. You need to be afraid of me, Tia. You need to keep a respectful distance and never be alone with me again."

He gave her a little shake before pushing her away. A cold draught seemed to rush between their bodies, like a vengeful spirit.

Her eyes searched his face, but he refused to soften his expression. Let her be afraid of him, fear his lusts and desires. Let her agonize over his secrets. They weren't suited, they would never agree, and she expected too much of him.

Far, far too much.

"So." He took a sustaining breath. "I'll be traveling to London shortly. I have an elderly aunt who's expressed a desire to see me. I could be gone some time. Please don't take any liberties with Polly in my absence. I don't mean her to be miserable, believe me, but I don't want her to have too much leeway either, or she'll take advantage. I mean her to grow up into a young woman with a character so blameless, she'll never suffer censure on account of her parents, or her past. Now, if that's all, I've business to attend to."

He dragged open the door, skinning his knuckles on the wood in his haste. Relishing the pain, he strode away.

How he'd allowed Tia so close to his heart, he didn't know.

She mustn't get any closer. Absenting himself from Foxleaze was the best way to achieve that end for now. Afterward, he'd return to exactly what he'd been before her arrival, and if she didn't like it . . .

Well, he'd have to give their future arrangements serious consideration.

Chapter 22

The first thing Tia did after Hal left for London was pen a letter to Lucy, Duchess of Finchingfield. Though increasing with Finchingfield's second child, Lucy had accompanied her husband to the capital, despite it being the end of the Season. As she'd informed Tia in an earlier letter, she loved him so much, she'd far rather be with, than without him.

Tia knew exactly what she meant. More so, now she was falling for Hal.

When she watched his carriage disappear down the drive, it was as if part of her had been hacked away—leaving her in agony.

Foolish, foolish girl, wasting her affections on a most undeserving man—one flawed beyond redemption. A fact made particularly obvious by the way he'd behaved toward her before he left.

The letter to Lucy was written and posted immediately afterward, in hopes it would reach London before Ansford did. Tia had charged Lucy with a mission and needed to give her friend time to engineer a meeting between her husband and Hal.

Without confessing her burgeoning attraction to him, Tia had asked Lucy to write back quickly if Finchingfield noticed any improvement in Hal. The Duke had attended the late Baroness Ansford's funeral and so would have been present on the cusp of Hal's descent into melancholia so severe, it verged on madness.

If the duke *did* notice a change for the better, it would

cheer Tia enormously to think she'd contributed. But it wasn't only her pride needing the boost. It was her heart.

If, while in London, Hal reverted to his dour, reclusive self, any improvement she'd wrought in him could be no more than skin deep. She'd have to give up all hope of happiness if this was the case.

She and Mama would then have to leave Foxleaze. She couldn't bear it if Hal were to treat her with the same indifference as when they'd first met.

She'd rather die.

Four days passed, but Tia heard nothing back from Lucy. She tried to convince herself if there were anything terribly wrong with Hal, her friend would have let her know instantly. So, there remained cause for hope.

She told herself the longer Hal remained in London, keeping company with his peers and his relations, the more likely he was to return to normality. His sojourn with his Aunt Dorothea might even work to Polly's advantage, for surely the woman would inquire after her great-niece, and might even prevail upon Hal to bring the girl up to Town on his next visit. Polly would love that.

It was now Sunday, another fine July day. After all religious duties had been attended to, Tia was left with time on her hands.

A perfect day to take Polly sketching. Only partly for pleasure, for it was still a lesson of sorts, and Tia didn't see how Hal could object.

"Where are we going, Miss Wyndham?" Polly asked as they donned their sunbonnets.

"Down to the river. Have you ever tried to draw water before?"

"You can draw water? Really?"

"Well, a representation of it, anyhow. But if it proves too difficult, there may be a kingfisher, or a water vole, or some interesting plant."

Polly pulled a face. "I had far rather draw a plant—I know how they work. A stem, leaves, flowers—simple. Voles and birds never stop moving."

"You must view them as a challenge. Observe closely and sketch while you can recall what you see. You may at least capture the essence of the animal, even if you can't record the detail."

Polly seemed unconvinced, but asked politely, "Do you think I might sit on the lawn if I put my apron beneath me?"

"Only if the grass isn't wet. Otherwise, we shall make do with the fallen tree trunk."

It seemed odd, on a well-run estate like Foxleaze, that the dead lime tree had never been taken away. But it made an admirable seat, with its trunk resting on the riverbank and the outer branches overhanging the rushing water. The latter made an excellent perch for kingfishers.

"What's that, Miss Wyndham?" Polly had set down her paint box and was pointing at the place where the great trunk forked. Nestled in the joint, in a damp mossy depression, grew a plant with bright green leaves. "Is the tree growing again?"

"Unlikely." Tia leaned out as far as she could and looked. "It may be a fern of some kind, growing out of the dead wood. I'm really not sure. I can see more than one, I think."

"Can I pick it and press it in my book? It looks most unusual."

"But it's out of reach."

"Oh, please, Miss Wyndham."

Tia gave a sigh of resignation. Her charge was clearly losing respect for her, trying to influence her with fluttering eyelashes and a simpering tone. From whom had she learned such a trick? As if she couldn't guess.

"I'll get it for you. I don't want you falling in." Gathering up her skirts, she clambered onto the trunk where the riverbank seemed most shallow and started edging out toward the plants.

It was farther than she expected, and she didn't want to trust her weight to the old branches, so she lay flat along the trunk and inched forward on her stomach. She was at full stretch, her fingers brushing the green fronds, when a great shout smote her ears.

Glancing back in alarm, she saw Hal bowling down the slope toward them, looking thunderous. She gave a great gulp of surprise, started to retreat, slipped down the curved trunk of the tree, and landed with a splash in the water.

Chapter 23

Hal's heart contracted when Tia fell in. His feet flew across the turf, and he tore off his jacket as he raced to the riverbank, almost tripping over the kitten, who seemed to think this was some kind of game.

When he saw his daughter's anxious face, Hal forced the fear from his own. "Polly, your kitten's come down to find you. Pick him up, so he doesn't fall in too. I'll rescue Miss Wyndham. Don't worry."

Casting off his shoes, he slithered down the bank, then used the trunk as a guide to find Tia. By the time he'd waded out where it was deep enough to swim, she'd emerged, spluttering and disorientated. Summoning all his strength, he made a single lunge for her before she could submerge again.

After a brief struggle—and a few unwelcome mouthfuls of water—he set her upright and stabilized his own footing. He pulled her against his body and rubbed frantically at her back to ease her coughing.

"I'm all right, Hal. You can release me now. My feet are touching the bottom."

Taking her by the shoulders, he held her away from him. Thoroughly soaked, her hair hung in black tendrils down her face, her thin gown plastered to her breasts like a second skin. His hands went up to her cheeks, brushing the hair away, and he rested his forehead for a brief moment against her brow. "Foolish, idiotic girl. Are you trying to drown yourself? It would surprise me greatly to learn you can swim."

"I've seen it done. I know the principle."

"But what on earth possessed you to crawl along the tree like that?" His hands slid from her shoulders down her arms, needing to reassure himself she was still all there. Her stubborn spirit hadn't been dampened by her experience.

Unfortunately.

"I was picking a fern. It was perfectly safe—if you hadn't suddenly bawled at me like that and given me a fright, I wouldn't have fallen in."

His fingers tightened. The urge to shake her was powerful, the desire to kiss her even stronger. She glared mulishly back at him until a small voice from the riverbank called, "Miss Wyndham?"

Hal glanced up to see Polly hovering anxiously above them, the struggling kitten in her arms. "It's all right, my dear," he called. "I'll have Miss Wyndham out directly. She's rather wet but otherwise, I believe, unharmed."

"Polly, don't worry. Hal," Tia added in a softer voice, "you can let go of me now."

"I certainly will not. Do you think you can flounder out on your own, in a waterlogged dress? You weigh a good deal more now than you did when you went in, and the bank is muddy. I'll lift you onto the tree so you can work your way back along it."

Hal kept an arm about her waist as they pushed against the sluggish current, and hefted her up onto the trunk, where he was treated to the sight of her delectable derriere wriggling about as she tried to settle herself safely.

His body reacted swiftly and decisively, catching him completely off-guard. He bit down hard on his lip, willing his painfully throbbing member into abeyance. He could *not* emerge from the water in his present state.

Tia had shuffled along the trunk until she reached level ground and now stood upright on the bank, trying to squeeze the water from her hair while Polly bustled about behind her, wringing out the bottom of her dress. The water had molded the muslin to Tia's form so perfectly, nothing was left to the imagination.

He almost groaned aloud. With the white dress detailing every curve and dip of her body, and her arms uplifted to her flowing hair, her pert nipples pressing against the wet cloth, she was every inch the image of her namesake. Galatea, a marble statue of a woman so beautiful, King Pygmalion had fallen in love with it and begged for it to be given life.

His manhood jerked painfully against the constriction of his sodden breeches. "Miss Wyndham," he called in a strangled voice. "Please cover yourself. Use my jacket—it's on the ground behind you. Go straight up to the house and change."

"Why? It's warm enough for me to dry out here if I wring myself out. Anyway, we're waiting for you."

They might have a long wait. He cursed softly and started unbuttoning his waistcoat, steadying his footing against the river's flow.

"What are you doing, sir?"

"Since I'm already soaked, I thought I might as well have my swim now. I missed it while in London."

Both members of his audience stared at him as if he were mad, but he removed the garment and tossed it upon the bank, then leaned against the tree for support while he took off his ruined stockings. The shirt would be an encumbrance, but there were too many interested eyes upon him, so he remained inside it.

"I'm going to swim up and down for a bit. Go back to the house, both of you. Miss Wyndham, you really must change out of your wet things. I don't want you becoming ill."

Expecting to be obeyed, he reached for the middle of the river with long, powerful strokes, putting all his energy into the act of swimming to force his thoughts away from the act of making love.

Gradually the flowing water cooled and calmed him, both mind and body, as it always did. Here he was free, at peace, all his sins and guilt washed away by the current, along with responsibilities and cares.

When his limbs finally began to tire, he turned about and splashed his way back, heading for his usual bathing place by the willow tree, where the shallow bank was cleaner, and he was unlikely to be observed. But when he thrust out to avoid the dead tree at the site of the earlier near-catastrophe, he discovered the onlookers hadn't gone back to the house.

Good God! Would Tia *never* do as she was told?

Was he going to have to teach her a lesson?

Chapter 24

Coming to a halt by the tree, Hal grabbed onto it and growled, "Miss Wyndham, why have you not gone indoors?"

"Polly was afraid you might drown, so I let her watch you swim, to reassure her. *I've* found it quite instructive as well."

"You must dry yourself," he commanded, shaking the water from his hair. Why wouldn't the wretched woman ever listen to reason?

"I will, I will. I already have a bit," she assured him but made no sign of returning to the house.

Now his errant body was under control, he could ensure she went back indoors—on his shoulder if necessary. He scrambled up onto the tree trunk to avoid getting muddy, used his bare toes to get a firm grip, and walked carefully along its length before leaping down onto terra firma.

A curious sight met his eyes. Tia had cast off his jacket from around her shoulders and was running in wide circles on the grass, flapping her skirts out in front of her to dry them. Polly skipped along in her wake, clearly enjoying this diversion from lessons, and her kitten—who evidently liked the new game—chased around their feet in an apparent effort to trip them up.

He became aware of an unaccustomed tension in his stomach, spine, and shoulders. With a painful shudder, the pressure burst out through his lungs, and he laughed aloud.

Once he began, he couldn't stop. His sides ached, the tears rolled down his cheeks, and his gut clenched and unclenched in an unremitting spasm until he feared he was about to shatter.

A gulp of air turned into a sob, followed by another, wracking his whole body. Hal pressed his hands against his face, deeply humiliated. Through the maelstrom of emotions, he heard Tia's voice. "Polly, take your kitten into the house and feed him. Afterward, you can go back to the nursery and read for half an hour before luncheon. Your father is perfectly well. Only, he's laughed too much at our silly antics and needs time to recover. Go."

The sound of scurrying footsteps accompanied Tia's arm winding about his heaving shoulders as her soft body pressed against his side. He leaned toward her and grasped the fingers that curved against the muscle of his upper arm, struggling for control.

The sobs continued, but they sounded more like hiccups now.

What a fool I'm making of myself. In front of Tia, too.

For three years he'd stored up this agony. During those years he'd tried to be strong. Grieving, yes, but dry-eyed, for gentlemen never wept. Especially not those of noble birth.

Hal sucked in a trembling breath. He ought to behave like a man and release the warm, delicate fingers he held. But they offered a comfort he hadn't known for an exceedingly long time.

"It's all right, Tia, I'm all right," he managed. "I'm not distressed, truly. It's just that I haven't laughed at all since Mary's death."

Her breath brushed his cheek. "I know you haven't, Hal. I know you haven't. But it was high time, wasn't it?"

He grimaced. "I dare say it was."

"And they do say, don't they, sometimes you laugh until you cry? I imagine the body can't help it."

Dear, sweet girl. He didn't deserve her sympathy, or her commiseration—he'd used her ill, yet here she sat, forgiving him, condoling with him. With an almighty effort, he eased her away and got to his feet, pulling her up after him.

"You'd best not hold me again in public," he warned. "We don't want to give the servants something to gossip about."

"I don't care about the servants. I want you to be happy."

His heart gave a kick. She cared about his happiness? This was a precious gift indeed, and most unexpected. "Don't worry about me. But I genuinely don't want any of my staff seeing us in our present sodden state if it can be avoided."

Hal couldn't help but glance down at her body. The cloth clung to her in an obscenely provocative fashion, stoking his blood to fever heat.

"Here, put my jacket back on." His voice was harsh. Collecting the rest of his clothing, he pulled her away from the water, into the lee of the folly tower.

"If we cross from here to the archway and the cloisters, we can make it up the back stairs to my suite without being seen. One of my dressing gowns will cover you head to foot so that you can return to your own wing with dignity."

It wasn't really her dignity he was worried about. It was his self-control, now drawn out gossamer-thin. When they eventually reached the protective shadow of the archway unobserved, he sent up a silent prayer of thanks.

As soon as they were safely inside his dressing room, he locked the door and turned to his fellow conspirator. Her chest rose and fell rapidly as she regained her breath from their run, and his eyes snagged once again on those delectable curves.

God help him. If he could send her back to her mama without ravishing her first, he deserved a medal. Setting his teeth against the pull of temptation, he grabbed a dressing gown and handed it to Tia, then turned his back and sent out yet another silent prayer.

This time, he prayed for strength.

Chapter 25

Tia's chest heaved with delicious wickedness after their run across the grass. She was now locked in Hal's chamber.

Alone with him.

She took the robe he thrust at her and shrugged into it. It pressed her wet gown against her skin, chilling her. Pulling a face, she threw it off again and went behind his dressing screen.

He spun around. "Tia, what are you doing?"

"I'm going to change out of my horrid wet things before I put this on. Have you a towel I can use?"

"Tia, no. Put the dressing gown back on and go to your room. I command it."

She pulled at the hooks on her dress. "You don't command me, Hal. You can ask politely, like a gentleman. It's high time someone corrected your manners."

"If you undress in my chamber, my manners are your least concern. Don't you know about desire?"

Yes, she knew all too well. She'd thought about it a great deal in his absence. And was interested to learn more. As much as she could, in fact.

Slipping out of her dress, she spread it over the screen, trying to smooth out the creases. "Am I to presume you desire me?" She gazed at him over the top of the wooden panels.

He paused, arms tangled in the shirt he was currently peeling off and scowled at her. "You should never ask a man that question—it could be construed as an invitation. It's most improper for us to discuss such things."

The shirt was defeated and cast onto a chair. When he reached for his spare dressing gown, she knew an enormous sense of disappointment. Ducking her head, she applied herself to her lacings and swiftly removed her stays, shift, and petticoat.

Oh, how good it was to be out of the cloying, damp stuff. But she was sticky with moisture, and goosebumps erupted across her skin. "The towel, Hal, if you please."

She peeped above the screen again and saw with a quiver of anticipation that his soaked breeches had now joined his shirt. Clutching a robe around his body, he picked up a towel and padded barefoot across the rug toward her.

It was at that point she remembered he was actually a head taller than herself and would be able to look over the screen at her nakedness. She lurched forward and pressed herself against the painted wood, praying he'd throw the towel to her without coming any closer.

Her prayer went unheeded. He came to within an inch of the screen, until she was staring up at him. His eyes were so dark they were almost black, the seam between his lips a deep line of shadow. Still damp from its soaking, his hair had lost all its golden sheen, and clung in waves about his face, accentuating the strong, masculine lines. His expression was positively hungry. No, *ravenous*.

She quailed but refused to back off, knowing he could see nothing but the bare skin of her neck and shoulders from this position. Hopefully, her unbound hair shielded her.

The screen rocked as he pushed his body against it from the other side. Looking determined, he placed both hands on top, on a level with her face.

He was going to tear it down and expose her in her nakedness.

Tia's breath hitched. She hadn't meant to be quite so provocative. The fact the man had wept for his dead wife didn't make him any less of a man. His virility was undiminished, his basic urges unaffected.

Keep looking at his eyes, Tia, keep looking at his eyes. Put on your most disapproving face, and he'll back down.

The screen tipped, and she grabbed for the top, holding on for dear life.

Hal smiled. Not the heart-blistering, dazzling benediction she'd seen before, but a greedy, leonine grin. In a minute he would be licking his lips like an animal before a feast. She was achingly aware of his body on the other side of the thin woodwork, his heat penetrating the panels. A mere fraction of an inch separated her quaking body from his.

Her heart sped up. Why was he was no longer covered by his dressing gown? That could *not* have happened by accident.

Enslaved by his fevered gaze, she stood breathless as he pressed his fingers between her own. When his eyes released hers, his attention fastened on her mouth. She wet her lips and clasped his fingers tightly.

Finally, wonderfully, he kissed her. At first only her forehead, and her closed eyelids—hot, searing kisses that made her feel beautiful and desirable. She stood on tiptoe, tilting her face, her entire body throbbing with danger and excitement.

He found her mouth. The pressure of those firm, masculine lips made her ache with yearning. She whimpered and pressed her own against his, and he angled his head, allowing her to taste more of him.

His kiss hinted at sinful pleasures, and she was desperate to learn more. She pulled away to appreciate the masculine beauty of his mouth, then leaned in to run her tongue across the heated flesh, tracing the contours of his tantalizing lips. He compelled her, fascinated her, tempted her to explore what he had to offer.

Only, she needed him to show her what to do.

He eased his hands free and cupped her face, his lips bearing down on hers as if he meant to hurt her, but the pressure was raw pleasure, and she twined her arms around his neck to stop him moving away.

Her erect nipples now rasped against the roughness of the wood in an overwhelmingly erotic fashion, and she tried to imagine what it would be like to rub them against Hal's hot, hard body. Suddenly she wanted the screen gone, wanted it to take fire from the heat of their bodies and burn to instant ash so they could be naked and unashamed in each other's embrace.

She moaned softly as he dug his hands into her hair and increased the pressure of his kiss. When her lips parted again, his tongue drove in hard, and as her own tongue tangled with his, flames of desire leapt in her belly, stoked by the depth and intensity of his kiss.

This was heaven. More staggering than she could ever have imagined—and she'd imagined quite a lot where he was concerned. Death, loss, deprivation, misery—all these things were swept away in the passion of the moment. Nothing else existed but the two of them, a man and a woman lost in the joy of arousal, consumed by the pleasures of the flesh.

He kissed her again with a bold certainty that thrilled her. A moment later, as if by magic, the screen was gone, and she was pressed up against the entire firm, deliciously naked length of him.

Before she had time to appreciate the shockingly sinful sensation, he scooped her up in his arms and carried her through the connecting doorway into his bedchamber.

Chapter 26

What was he going to do? Tia shivered with delicious imaginings.

"Forgive me, Tia," Hal whispered as he laid her down on the bed, "I want you more than I can bear. I don't want to hurt you, I don't want to take advantage of you, but I can hardly control myself. My self-imposed celibacy was, it seems, a mistake. I'm hungry for you. I need you to help me be strong."

"If you want to deny yourself, why am I on your bed?"

He seemed taken aback. Hardly surprising, since her voice sounded like deep velvet. She'd almost purred the words.

"Because I want to see what you look like, naked and aroused, your hair spilling out across the pillow, your eyes dark with longing for me. I'm an artist, Tia. The portrait in my study is my own work. I need to sketch you, paint you, pay homage to your beauty, of both person and character. But I can't expect you to pose for a nude, so I want to steal this chance to admire you before you return to your room."

"Why can't you expect me to pose?" She ran her eyes greedily across the firmly-muscled contours of his body. *He* was the beautiful one, surely, not she.

"Because observing you naked, for the time it takes to create a sketch, would be temptation beyond endurance. I can barely contain my response to you now. Imagine my suffering if I have to examine you for an entire hour, exploring with my eyes each dip and rise of your form, detailing intimately every inch of you, your breasts, the cleft between your legs, and the curve of your bottom."

Tia shuddered in wanton anticipation at the image his words conjured up. Yes, she wanted him to do exactly that, examine every part of her with intimate precision, bring every yearning inch of flesh to aching awareness, magnifying the awareness with his hands, as well as his gaze.

"Hal, please. I'm not a living statue—I'm flesh and blood. When you kiss me, I never want it to stop. When you touch me, I want you to touch all of me."

He shook his head. "I cannot believe it. Tia, I'm so unworthy of you."

Not true. He wasn't perfect, but she loved him anyway, with her whole heart. If she told him she loved him, would it help him make up his mind?

Apparently, the expression on her face was all the invitation he needed.

Stretching out alongside her, he captured her mouth with his, kissing her until she thought she would swoon from the glory of it. Next, he started an insistent nibbling at her neck and her earlobe that sent frenzied shivers across her skin.

She wanted him to be kissing more of her. She was a mass of aching demands, her flesh eager for his hands, his mouth, the brush of his hair, his avid gaze.

Brazenly, she pushed a hand between them, reveling in the sinful delight of exploring his muscular torso, the firm flesh of his belly, and the intriguing pathway of dark hair tracking from his navel to his loins. Where her hand encountered an interesting development.

He dragged his mouth from her flesh. "I apologize for my unruly body's reaction." His voice was a hoarse rasp. "I seem to have no more dominion over it than I have over *you*, Miss Galatea Wyndham."

He ran a finger down her collarbone to her navel, brushing his wrist across one nipple as he went. His finger returned to describe lazy circles around the beaded peak, teasing her mercilessly. When he wet his finger and stroked her sensitive tip, she moaned and arched toward his hand.

Leaning down, he applied his mouth to her aching nipple. Her body clenched and shuddered as she rolled toward him, wanting to press herself once more against his alluring, masculine body, with all of its power and its promise. But his arm held her down, so he could give his full attention to her other breast.

It didn't seem fair he should be giving so much pleasure to her and receive none himself. Tia worked her fingers into the curly hair above the juncture of his thighs and fastened them around his engorged manhood.

His sharp intake of breath gave her pause. "Oh, I'm so sorry. Have I hurt you?"

"Not at all. I'm surprisingly durable in certain places. If you explore any lower, however, I would ask you to be gentle."

His mouth sought hers again, and she savored the sensation of running her hand up and down his shaft in time with the thrusting of his tongue. He groaned, pushing against her until she rubbed harder, before probing delicately at the silken tip.

He gasped. "Too much, Tia, too soon. Have pity on me. I can't control myself if you touch me like that—I'll spill my seed."

She flushed at his frankness, then laughed at her absurdity. "Would that be a terrible thing?"

"It would be if I'd not yet had the pleasure of being inside you."

He wanted to be inside her? How did that work, exactly?

Pressing her close, he kissed her again and pushed one hand between her legs.

"You're wet," he breathed.

Wet? What did he mean? "I'm sorry," she murmured against his neck.

He pulled back and looked at her, puzzled. Then his face cleared and he treated her to another of his heartwarming grins. But this one was boyishly wicked. The effect on her was so profound, she was tempted to tell him she loved him.

But what he did next sent her thoughts in another direction entirely.

He stroked and probed the soft folds of flesh in her most private of parts until his questing finger found and massaged a place whose sensitivity had her virtually sobbing with arousal and need.

"Hal." She dug anxious fingers into his shoulders. "What's happening?"

"Don't be afraid." He drew his lips across hers in a searing benediction. "It's meant to be like this. I'm making sure you're ready for me, as my self-control is about to fall off the cliff-edge. We both need fulfilment-right here, right now."

The pulsing action of his finger made her squeeze her legs together to increase the incredible sensation, but he ruthlessly pushed them apart again and shifted his body, so he was suspended above her, resting on his forearms.

The nub of his proud manhood pushed at the place where his hand had been, before slipping inside her.

She glanced up anxiously when his pressure met her resistance, but the expression of wonder on his face soothed her, so she forced her body to relax. Suddenly, after a sharp nip of pain, he was filling her, every delectable inch of him, pushing up inside her, being welcomed by her body. Her heart skidded to a halt, waiting, loving the sublime expression on his face.

He began to move, pulling out slowly, while she contracted around him, eking out every bit of pleasure as the friction built between them. He pushed in again, groaning under his breath. And repeated the action, setting up a series of exhilarating vibrations in her womb that almost overwhelmed her.

He lowered his hips and delved more deeply, increasing the speed and power of his movements, heightening her enjoyment with every thrust, to her very core.

"Lift for me." His breath came in quick gasps. "I want to feel every inch of you."

She obeyed, curling her spine and changing the angle between them. As he delved in again, the pressure of his body urged her legs farther apart, and he took full advantage, filling her completely. She rose up to meet his plunging body with hers, adding her moans of pleasure to his.

Each stroke brought him closer to her, each advance and retreat sealing the bond between them until she could no longer think of him as a separate being. His desires were the same as hers, he moved to the same pulse she did, and she met each thrust in perfect time, her pleasure escalating beyond imagination.

Abruptly his rhythm collapsed, and Tia was lost somewhere in the firmament while a million explosions of ecstasy filled her womb. She tilted her head back and gave a cry, never before having been so at one with herself, with Nature and the stars—and with her superlative lover.

His chest heaving, a sheen of sweat covering his brow, Hal clasped her close despite the heat trapped between their bodies, holding her as if she were the most cherished thing in his entire universe.

"Are you in pain, my love?" His breath was ragged.

"Quite the opposite."

He bent to her and kissed her smiling lips while she ran a hand along the slick flesh of his back, enjoying the ripple of muscle she found there.

The floodgates had been opened, their lust sated. She'd been utterly ruined by her employer.

Tia had enjoyed every last second of it.

Chapter 27

Two weeks had passed since Hal had made love to Tia, and he was a changed man. Life had accepted him back, there was a spring in his step, and the folly had been forgotten.

All he needed to do now was curb his insatiable desire for her and set about the task of winning her heart.

This he was unlikely to do without making an offer of his own. But was he ready to raze the fortress he'd constructed around his heart after Mary?

Despite the joy that bubbled up at the idea of making Tia irrevocably his, he continued to be beset by doubts. They had yet to come to any consensus about Polly. He wasn't sure he was ready to reveal to Tia the grim secrets of his marriage and Mary's death, and he had also to win Sarah Wyndham around. She, although polite enough, clearly neither fully understood nor trusted him.

Worst of all, if Hal wanted to court Tia in the traditional way—and he did, very much—she would no longer be able to live beneath the same roof as himself. So, in order to win her, he ought to let her go.

But how could he bear her absence?

He rapidly discovered, however, why Society had laid such a rule upon its upper echelons. It took all the *sang froid* he could muster to treat Tia normally in front of her mother and Polly. He was forced to avoid being alone with her, for fear of falling upon her like a ravening wolf, and rapidly removing all barriers between them.

The situation was intolerable. But he couldn't think of a solution that would please either of them. Thus, he'd taken to ever more frequent cooling dips in the river, and increasingly bruising rides around his estate.

A gallop around the bounds was what he needed right now. It was late July, and after a spell of light summer rain, the weather had cleared. He could take Juniper out and tear across Haden's pasture, perhaps come back along the lane via the village. Afterward, he would have tea and refreshment with Tia.

His mind conjured up a vision of her face, recalling the delightful way her lips curled up at each corner, the Cupid's bow of her mouth, and the angle and straightness of her nose. He imagined her eyes, their warm honey-brown color, mellowing into something deeper when she gazed at him. As if she were right before him now, he could see her black lashes and silky eyebrows, charmingly arched, giving her a quizzical appearance. He grinned as he pictured the soft arc between chin and throat—the jaw determined, like its owner.

He strode across the cobbles of the stable yard and cast an eye around the carriage lodge. Then looked again. His pleasure faded.

"Michaels!" he called to the head groom, who was leading Juniper out to meet him. "What happened to the Stanhope?"

"I believe Miss Wyndham took it out to give Miss Pelham a run around the lanes, my lord."

Hal's whip clattered to the cobbles. "Miss Wyndham can drive?"

"I don't know, sir, but the young lady wasn't driving today."

Panic slammed into him. "Who the deuce was?"

"A gentleman called Mr. Leigh. He informed me he was a friend of Mr. Brooks, he whose father is Member of Parliament for—"

"Yes, yes, I know who his blasted father is."

Tia had taken Polly for a carriage ride, without his permission? In the company of a young man? His shock gave way to fury. "What direction did they take?"

"Toward the village, sir."

After the village, the road led along the valley to Chippenham.

Chippenham? He smacked his fist against his thigh. Of course. Today was the day of the fair she'd been begging him to attend.

A thousand curses on the woman. Not only had she gone without his permission, but she'd also abducted Polly. What was she thinking, taking Leigh as her escort? It was highly improper. Could she not have taken Lynch, or Aldergate instead?

Completely unacceptable. He couldn't allow his future wife to attract the attention of the tabbies by gallivanting off with a young man he'd never even met. Perhaps it was as well he hadn't yet proposed to her. Evidently more taming was required.

Seizing his whip from the ground, Hal leapt onto the mounting block and straddled his horse. "Thank you, Michaels. That will be all. Juniper, on."

He was going after her.

And Lord preserve her when he caught up with her.

Chapter 28

Hal's stallion had a magnificent turn of speed cross-country, so that was the way he chose to ride until he reached the turnpike. He slowed down there, to protect the animal's hooves—but even so, he managed to overtake his Stanhope gig before it reached the town.

The gig had come to a standstill, mired in the increased traffic, and as Hal was on horseback, he had little difficulty weaving through to confront its occupants.

"Miss Wyndham, Polly. Mr. Leigh, I don't believe we've met." He touched a finger to his beaver hat and was pleased at the startled look on the young man's face. Devil take him, he was a handsome rogue, currently managing the ribbons admirably in the crush. Hal's fingers whitened on Juniper's reins.

Ideally, he should drag the fellow out of his seat and throttle him. Tia would need to be castigated too. But preferably not in public.

He flushed as he leaned down from the saddle, saying as coolly as he could, "I believe there's been a misunderstanding, Mr. Leigh. I'm the Hon. Miss Pelham's father. As such, *I* was supposed to be taking her to the fair today."

Even though Hal kept his voice down, he became aware of people staring. Much as he would have liked to call Leigh out, he could hardly do it in front of so many witnesses, nor could he physically assault the fellow, as the fury banked within his breast urged him to do. He clung to his patience and waited, steadfastly refusing to acknowledge the treacherous Tia any further.

Leigh doffed his hat as his Adam's apple bobbed nervously. "Your pardon, my lord. I came around to deliver a book to Miss Wyndham we'd talked about while dining at the Douglas mansion, but found her in a distracted state."

"Distracted state?"

"Indeed. She'd promised Miss Pelham a trip to the fair and told me you were to have accompanied them but were taken ill with severe dyspepsia after an over-indulgence of St. John's Wort. I trust you're rather better now, my lord."

Dyspepsia? St. John's Wort?

My goodness, but I'm going to give Tia a talking-to when I get her home!

"I find I am much recovered, sir." Hal struggled to keep the choler out of his tone. "Quite well enough to carry out my initial commission. So, your services are no longer required."

Leigh seemed about to protest. Hal kept his face carefully blank but raised one eyebrow the tiniest fraction.

The young man took the hint. "Miss Wyndham, Miss Pelham." Leigh tipped his hat to the ladies as he clambered down from his seat.

Sensible young man.

Hal slid easily from Juniper's saddle and reached into his pocket. "Here's a shilling, Mr. Leigh, so you can find someone to take my stallion back to his stable. After that you may continue on your way—I believe it's no more than a few hundred yards to the fair field. We can meet up with you there if you wish to walk around with us. Unless you'd prefer to ride Juniper back to Foxleaze yourself, and abandon your plans?"

Leigh cast an anguished glance at Tia, who appeared extremely self-conscious, then gazed up at Hal's magnificent black stallion. Faced with the choice between a swift carefree gallop across the fields, and a ramble around Chippenham

Fair with an irate baron, the young man took the only viable option.

With a grim smile of satisfaction, Hal helped him aboard Juniper, received his shilling back again, and climbed into the wide seat of the Stanhope.

He cast a quelling glance at Tia and received a haughty toss of the head in return. The horses lurched forward as the traffic began moving once again, forcing him to concentrate on driving. It was impossible to reprimand his companions without attracting the attention of the crowd. His harangue must wait for a private moment.

Clicking his tongue in annoyance, he hunched forward and tried to identify the best route. It was no mean feat navigating his rig between the loaded goods wagons and pack-horses, and the pedestrians with their accompanying hens, children, and baskets. Fortunately, he was an experienced driver, even though he was used to tooling along in rather grander equipages than the gig.

Above the babble of talk, laughter, honks, as well as grunts and mooing, he was able to catch something of what was happening on the seat behind him. Polly was thoroughly excited, pointing at anything that caught her eye, and bombarding Tia with questions about it. Virtually everyone they encountered was offered a greeting. Each time his daughter announced to complete strangers, "My papa is taking us to the fair, isn't it thrilling," Hal winced with embarrassment.

The last thing he wanted was to attract any more attention.

Being who he was, however, it was inescapable. Some of the people hereabouts remembered him from when he'd maintained a far more public profile—and were keen to greet him.

Confound it. If only he'd kept the long hair and beard, he might have escaped their notice, for he loathed indulging in small talk. Yet, bit by bit, the pain of greeting people and touching his hat to them started to recede, and he found himself responding with a cheerful nod, which seemed to satisfy everyone.

Nonetheless, it was with considerable relief that he finally brought the gig to a halt and paid a dubious-looking man to mind it—at the same time, silently cursing Tia for not coming out with one of the grooms. Barely was this business concluded than Tia and Polly were out of the cart and heading toward the fair field. With a sigh of resignation, he strode off in their wake.

Chippenham Fair was largely a country event, dealing in sheep, cattle, pigs, fowl, and fodder. Hal allowed himself a moment's pleasure at seeing the fat, healthy animals and the cheerful faces of the country folk. Every rustic delight imaginable was on offer, from great casks of cider and clove-stuck hams to mutton pies and freshly-roasted hog.

Entertainment was also available in abundance. Balladeers, poets, musicians demonstrating the cheerful sound of the hurdy-gurdy and hautbois, plied their talent alongside fortune tellers and Romany dancers.

He stood at Tia's elbow while Polly gazed in mute fascination at a marionette show.

"You have behaved very badly," he whispered in Tia's ear.

"And you, Hal, are a hypocrite, for you, too, have behaved badly."

True. But at least he hadn't made a public spectacle of himself. Though the day was yet young.

"Maybe. But at least I'm prepared to apologize and make amends. I sense no such repentance in yourself."

She stared straight ahead, her mouth set primly. "I gave you ample opportunity and reason to allow Polly to come to the fair. You chose not to listen."

"I believe I'm permitted to lay down the law in my own house," he retorted.

"Not when the law is wrong. Besides, when you let other people into your life, you must expect to have to compromise."

Also true, but these things took time. He'd been isolated for too long. "Can you not compromise too, Tia? I've asked little else of you."

She turned to him, her brown eyes flashing. "*Little else*? We're not allowed to sing, you won't come to church with us, we don't have visitors, and Polly never gets to play with anyone her own age."

He bristled at this. "I never forbade you to have visitors. I merely chose not to be involved if you did."

"And who's going to come, knowing you're too dismal to speak with them?" she countered, warming to her subject.

He wasn't dismal. Not anymore, and he had her to thank for it. But the thoughts and emotions swirling inside his head and heart were newly-born, making him vulnerable. He needed more time.

"You know I'm not yet fit for company. I'd only spoil your get-togethers."

"I can't disagree."

Her words stung his fragile heart like a lash. He averted his head to hide the hurt—

And discovered Polly had vanished.

Chapter 29

He grasped Tia's elbow. "Where's Polly?"

"Oh, my goodness, she was right in front of me only a minute ago. How could she disappear so quickly?"

He took one look at Tia's white, frightened face, and battened down his own fears to reassure her. "She can't be far. If you go right, I'll go left—and if you haven't found her in one-quarter of an hour, meet me back here, and we'll set a search in motion."

He didn't know how he managed to sound so calm when he was in such internal turmoil. It was most unlike him to panic, but the idea some harm might have befallen his daughter filled him with mind-numbing terror. Thrusting his way through the throng, he hunted for his child.

She can't have gone far, she can't have gone far. He'd only disputed with Tia for a moment. Why hadn't they commanded Polly not to go anywhere without them? Why had he not taken her hand?

Willing his heart into a steadier rhythm, Hal tried to think logically. If someone had abducted his daughter, they'd have made for the edge of the field, perhaps to where the carts and carriages were drawn up, in order to spirit her away quickly. He should have told Tia to search the stalls, while he searched the margins of the fair. What on earth was wrong with him? Why couldn't he think straight?

"Papa?"

He almost dropped to his knees. "*Polly?* Thank God, child. Where have you been?"

"I don't think you're supposed to blaspheme, Papa. They say so in church. And Miss Wyndham says so too."

"I thought I'd lost you." The urge to fold her to his breast was strong, but how would she respond to such an open display of emotion? If he wanted her to learn to control her emotions, he couldn't be prey to his own.

With inevitable childish logic, she replied, "I wasn't lost. I can find my way easily. I know exactly how to get back to the gig if I need to. And Miss Wyndham is wearing a bronze paisley shawl, so I can find her by her color, and you are a very tall person, so I can see you above other people's heads."

He kept his expression stern. "Not the point. You can't run off like that, Polly. It's extremely naughty."

"I'm sorry, Papa. I only peeped inside the fortune teller's booth for a moment to see her crystal ball, and when I came out again, you were gone. I'd only gone half a yard."

"It was at least half a dozen, my girl. Don't tell untruths."

"No, Papa. I really am very sorry." Her lower lip quivered, and tears glistened in the blue-gray eyes.

Hal groaned inwardly and softened his voice. "All right. Apology accepted. Don't do it again. And now we must find Miss Wyndham, before she, too, is lost."

"She isn't lost. I can see her by the stand with the red ribbons. Bronze paisley shawl—I told you."

Tia was soon reunited with her charge, and although she was decidedly businesslike in the way she dealt with the child, he could see she was as relieved as he was.

The stall with the red ribbons turned out to be selling—amongst other things—the juice of crushed raspberries and strawberries, albeit at an exorbitant cost. Polly, of course, had to have some, and he bought a cup for Tia too, secretly relishing the way it stained her lips a darker red, igniting wicked thoughts about the movement of her tongue as she licked it off.

Polly inevitably spilled some down her dress. Later on, she also tripped on a tent peg, bruised her foot, and got grass stains on her skirts. The fair was proving to be more hazardous than a battlefield, and he was certain someone had attempted to pick his pocket on more than one occasion.

"I pride myself on having managed to keep my temper thus far, Miss Wyndham, considering the numerous inconveniences of this outing. I'm yet to be convinced such activities can be construed as pleasant."

But Tia's spirits seemed indefatigable. "Really, sir? Don't tell me you've never been to a fair before."

"I assure you I haven't. I wish I had a guinea for every countrywoman who has banged my elbow with her basket today."

"You should try and participate instead of lurking around looking like you're sucking a lemon. Anyway, we're not here for *your* pleasure—we're here for Polly's."

"Where has she got to now? Oh, for heaven's sake, she's making for the dance-floor." In complete exasperation, he called out, "*Polly, no.* I forbid it."

"I'm sorry, Hal." Tia gave his elbow a squeeze. "I hadn't realized she would be quite so uncontrollable. I'd better go and rescue her."

He watched Tia make her way to the primitive staging erected on the most level part of the field. A group of musicians had struck up a lively air, and some of the younger fair-goers were already stamping their feet on the boards.

Tia, far from rescuing Polly, darted in amongst them, seized her charge's hands and swung her around in a large circle, grinning broadly.

The bare-faced cheek of the woman. Hal surged forward furiously, only to trip on the basket Tia had left down by his feet. What was he now, a servant to guard their baggage? A packhorse? Muttering ferociously, he picked up the basket and marched up to the staging, determined to take control of the situation.

The other onlookers must have sensed his bristling presence, for they gave him space—and a good view of the dancing. The couples had broken up and were now dancing with other people in their sets. Tia was being swung vigorously about by a young man in fustian breeches, and she was laughing back into his pleasant, sun-browned face. Hal chewed on the inside of his cheek. He wanted to put his fist in that face. Some other fellow seized Tia—a much older gentleman this time, but equally unsuitable.

The basket handle creaked from the pressure of his fingers. Thankfully the music had ceased. But the dancers showed no sign of leaving the floor, and almost immediately the fiddle struck up another, even faster melody. Polly was scooped up by a jovial-looking boy, while a dark-haired man with silver buttons and a striped waistcoat bowed in front of Tia.

The basket hit the ground with a thud. Hal leapt onto the stage, swept the fellow aside, and grasped Tia by both hands. "Come away now," he hissed. "You're making a spectacle of yourself."

"No." She pulled him toward her in time with the music, then pushed him away again. "*You* are making a spectacle of *both* of us. Now dance. I'll tell you the steps—if I can remember them."

This was intolerable. But people had blocked him in on every side, so he had no alternative but to comply.

Never taking his eyes off her, he worked through the measure—and was bumped into and had his toes trodden on. His dignity was truly shattered when a large woman wearing an appalling bonnet lost her balance and collapsed into his arms.

Tia, damn her, laughed. As did Polly, the woman, and everyone else who noticed. When he glanced around, he discovered lots of people were losing their balance, making mistakes and guffawing about it. Clearly, dignity had no meaning at a dance at a rural fair.

He thought about the chilly, formal affairs he'd attended in the ballrooms of the *ton*, the multitudinous rules, and interminable etiquette—and his mouth twitched. There were no such rules here, and everyone was enjoying being liberated. He was relishing holding Tia about the waist and swinging her around when the music stopped.

They came to a halt, breathless and grinning at each other.

"Papa? Will you dance with me now?"

He cast Tia a horrified look.

She avoided his gaze. "I'd better rescue our basket or the sweets and toys will be gone."

"Traitor," he murmured after her before taking his daughter's outspread hands and rejoining the set, struggling to mask his chagrin. But Polly was thoroughly enjoying herself, particularly because the difference in their heights meant he often had to propel her through the air, making her squeal in delight.

In his daughter's face, he could see what Mary must have been like when she was a child, full of joy and optimism, completely unaware she would meet an early and unexpected end. The familiar pain of loss and guilt clawed at his chest, but with every sinew of his being, he fought against them, for the sake of his child, for the sake of the lovely young woman observing them from the edge of the stage.

Someone tripped and cannoned into someone else, and for a moment the dance was in uproar and people burst into laughter as they collided with each other, turned the wrong way, and struggled to right themselves.

A small, breathless voice piped up, "I like it when you look like that, Papa."

"Am I looking happy? I shall cease this instant. It is most unbecoming for a gentleman of my status to look cheerful in a place such as this."

"No, I know you're joking with me." She poked him. "No, promenade right, Papa, promenade *right*."

Finally, the torment ended, and he was able to rejoin Tia. He raised an eyebrow, daring her to laugh at him.

Instead, he surprised an expression on her face that was *not* amusement. Were her brown eyes moist?

"Is there something wrong, Miss Wyndham?"

"No, no, not at all. I think we should go home now before Polly becomes tired and disagreeable." What was that odd catch in her voice?

"Is she as disagreeable as me?" he asked, hoping to restore Tia to her normal, playful self.

"No, sir. Impossible."

Excellent, an insult. Her good humor had returned. He hadn't liked the other expression—it reeked of despair and loneliness. What had rendered her thus at such a jovial time? Had she been reminded of the dismal days in Selbury Poorhouse?

They should leave, lest they all become tired and maudlin.

He held out his arm, expecting to be given the basket to carry, but instead found Tia had wrapped her hand about his elbow. It was a thrill to have her so close to him again.

He held out his other hand to relieve her of the basket, but suddenly that was occupied as well, by a smaller, decidedly sticky, hand. Polly grinned up at him winsomely, so he gripped her firmly, pressed Tia's hand against his ribs, and escorted them through the crowd.

Was this what it was like to be part of a genuine, loving family? Or was it only a fleeting moment, a memory to be treasured but not repeated? If only he could be sure he held

Tia's heart. If only he knew whether or not Polly could come to love her papa.

Yet, if he unlocked his heart, fully opened it to them both, wouldn't he be opening himself up to more pain?

Chapter 30

Being in love was a hard journey to make if one didn't know how the object of one's love felt. When Tia saw Hal unbend toward Polly at the fair, she knew she was well and truly smitten.

But what was supposed to happen now?

She wanted to spend every waking moment with him, to converse and spar with him, to bask in the glory of his smile—and to have him gaze at her the way he had when they'd made love.

It was madness, of course. How could she have fallen in love with someone she barely knew, who kept so many secrets from her, who was irascible and selfish, not to mention far above her touch? She longed for the company of Lucy, or any of her childhood friends. But the others had all drifted away when the Wyndhams were faced with penury.

How fickle the world could be. Tia was beginning to appreciate why Hal had decided to remove himself from it.

The only person she could ask about his feelings and intentions was Hal himself—the one person she had not the courage to ask, for fear of being rejected. How would she cope?

Maybe he *did* care for her in more than a physical way. But if he wasn't ready to disclose the fact, she'd best be patient. He was a complex man, and she didn't want to risk losing him by doing the wrong thing.

Consequently, if she wasn't going to go mad with frustration and uncertainty, she must find some diversion. An activity of benefit to Polly would do very well.

Having come up with what she considered a masterful plan, she went in search of Mama to see what she thought.

"An afternoon of tea and croquet?" Mama put down her embroidery and beamed broadly. "What a splendid idea. But do you think Henry will agree?"

"Surely he can't object to a handful of children and their nurses playing croquet on the lawn for a couple of hours? Mrs. Dunne positively danced on the spot when I mentioned the idea—I think she'd welcome the challenge of having more than the four of us to care for."

Her mother's eyes sparkled. "Had you better talk to the head gardener to make sure the grass is nice and short and the lawn rolled? We'll need some cards made up for the invitations. How will you know whom to invite?"

"Therein lies the challenge. But I'm sure if we ask the older servants, they'll be able to identify those children with whom Polly associated before her mama died."

"What about the village children? It would be as good as a fête for them."

"I fear Hal might draw the line at that." Tia wandered across to the window and peered out at the balmy July evening. There was a certain magic in the air this time of year when the days were so long, each sunset beautiful and prolonged. Purple clouds were beginning to gather on the horizon, perhaps a sign of rain heading their way. She wondered where Hal was now, and whatê he was doing.

"Why?" Mama persisted, breaking Tia's train of thought. "He was always a champion of the poor. I can't see why he'd object to helping those on his own threshold. When will you put the scheme to him? Or should *I* do it?"

"It's quite late. He may be lingering at his supper or taking a glass of port wine before he retires."

"I wonder why he won't come down and dine with us? He can bear our company at breakfast now, and even luncheon on occasion—but dinner, never."

"Perhaps the dining room holds some unpleasant memories," Tia suggested, half-seriously. "Or mayhap Hal turns into a were-beast after dark and wishes not to be seen."

Mama chuckled. "It would explain a good deal, would it not? Perhaps you shouldn't disturb him after all."

The long shadows outside now merged as the sun dipped behind the clouds, making it harder to see. Tia smiled and turned away from the window. "I'm sure I can find something made from iron for protection—or is it silver I need? I can take a fork from the dining room canteen."

"Better safe than sorry, my dear. Shall I await your return, in case you come to harm, and I need to send out the hue and cry?"

"No, don't wait up. I'll be quite safe. Who knows, Hal and I may even engage in a normal conversation."

Not that any conversation would be normal now, after what had passed between them. There would always be an undercurrent.

Closing the door behind her, she set off for Hal's side of the house and knocked softly on the door of his study.

No response. She worked her way along the darkened corridor, tapping gently at every door, even his bedchamber, but there was no sound. He had either retired early and was already fast asleep, or . . . Could he be back in the folly again? She thought she'd managed to distract him from whatever it was he got up to in there.

She screwed up her courage and made for the stairwell at the end of the passageway. There was one lantern burning in a niche at the top of the stairs, so she took it to light her way down into the shadowy cloisters.

Once again, she experienced unease, the idea of medieval specters made all the more a reality by the eerie way the light bounced off the grotesque and grinning heads on the roof bosses. She wished she hadn't imagined Hal turning into a werewolf—for here, islanded by impenetrable darkness and ancient strangeness, she could almost believe it possible.

She darted across to the archway and out onto the lawn.

There was light in the folly. It could only be Hal, surely?

Tia hesitated. By moving across the grass, heralded by her tiny pool of light, she would announce her presence and her vulnerability to all the night things that were abroad. She would also risk Hal's wrath by seeking him out at the folly.

A bat flitted past her head and slanted in beneath the archway. The trees soughed in the gentle night breeze and shivers ran across her skin, even though it was mild.

No, she couldn't let her courage fail her now. What kind of mother would she make for Polly if she was afraid of the dark?

A mother to Polly? Now from where had *that* thought sprung?

Don't get distracted, Tia. Lifting her head and her lantern high, she strode across the lawn toward the folly, hastened up the steps, and knocked heavily on the door. Next, she put her back against it and turned to face the night, to ensure nothing evil or untoward had sneaked across the grass in her wake.

For some moments she stood there, afraid she'd get no answer. Then, to her relief, she heard the door open behind her and turned at Hal's surprised voice. "Tia? Whatever are you doing here?"

"I'm so glad you answered. I was afraid you wouldn't open the door."

"Afraid?"

"I'm sure someone or something was watching me as I came across here."

"Foolish girl. No one's there."

It was a relief to hear the comfort in his tone, but he didn't invite her into the folly. Instead, in a notably obvious fashion, he pulled the door shut behind him, took the key from around his neck, and locked it.

"What do you want?" There was no anger in his voice. Hopefully, a positive sign, but clearly the folly remained forbidden territory.

Before she could respond, he took her hand. "I'll walk back to the house with you if you wish, but I'm sure you're not being watched. The dogs would have made a ruckus if there were an intruder. They have extremely good noses and know exactly who should be about and who should not."

Of course—she was being ridiculous. She took a deep breath, tried to steady her heartbeat . . . and failed. Hal had her hand captive in his. Did the wretched man have no idea what his touch was doing to her? A tremor of fear became a quiver of desire.

"Has something happened, my sweet?" His voice was soft.

She swallowed hard and forced her thoughts back into their proper channel. "I wanted to ask your permission for something. Can we descend before we talk?" Her knees had already weakened, a considerable problem on the steep, gritty stairway.

"Certainly. Shall we go for an evening stroll?"

He helped her down with a care bordering on chivalry. *Gracious.* Was this *really* the same man she'd seen on her arrival at Foxleaze, so devoid of emotion or interest, she'd believed him a hermit?

Refusing to allow her mind to stray down the path of lust again, she burst out, "Mama and I want to invite some of the local children to join us for a game of croquet one afternoon. Polly has had no company her own age since her mama died. I'm certain it would be good for her to practice sharing and taking turns, and maybe get involved in a bit of rough and tumble."

"In a stately game like croquet?"

She could barely see him in the darkness, but no doubt he'd raised a quizzical eyebrow, a gesture that made her insides melt. She gave no reply, unsure she could trust her voice.

"How many children?" He tucked her hand into the crook of his arm as they wandered back in the general direction of the house.

"Oh, I thought perhaps ten. No more."

"Let us reduce the number to five. I know how much children can make their presence felt. So, who will you invite and who will accompany them? Will you have Cook organize a picnic? What will you do if it rains?"

"So, you don't refuse me outright?"

"I'm finding it increasingly difficult to refuse you anything, Miss Galatea Wyndham."

The warmth in his voice, as he spoke her name, thrilled her. It seemed she might be on the verge of winning more than one battle here.

"We'll make sure everything is well planned. I want to cause you as little inconvenience as possible."

"I don't intend to be inconvenienced at all. I shall go out."

Up ahead in the darkness a duck muttered to itself. A tawny owl wafted past on silent wings.

"But you never go out." Tia tried to keep the disappointment from her voice.

"Except to London and fairs."

"Apart from those. I assumed they were exceptions to the rule."

"Not anymore. You've undermined all my rules, turned my life upside-down, driven me out of my refuge, forced me to cut my hair, and let me make a laughingstock of myself in front of the local peasantry. I don't know what to do with you, Tia. I don't know what to do without you, either."

The darkness hid her elation, but she thought she had never been happier than when she heard this confession fall from his lips.

Yet, until she knew the secret of the folly, she could never truly consider herself the victor.

Chapter 31

As he confessed his feelings to Tia, Hal inwardly begged Mary's forgiveness. It seemed—if no obstacle were to be found—he could now progress with his life. He could marry Tia, she would be a mother to Polly, and Mary's shade would drift back into the darkness, where it belonged. But not until he had completed his homage to her. Which he had no expectation of doing yet.

Tia's soft voice penetrated his musings. "It might please Polly if you were to join us. She'd be proud to present her Papa to her new friends."

He turned toward her and laid a hand on each shoulder, bringing his head close to hers. Her flesh welcomed his fingers, and her lips turned up to his, full of invitation.

"Tia." Their faces were so close he could smell the lavender scent of her hair. "You're always trying to push me too far. You know by now of the uncertainness of my temperament, that I can be as quick to condemn as I am to praise. You also know, with but little provocation, I will do unimaginably sinful things to your body. Have you no idea the power you exert on me? Why, even now, when we are talking about the most normal of things, I want to seize you in my arms and kiss you until you beg for mercy. Or expire, for lack of air."

She quivered in his grasp. He shook his head violently and retreated. "I've revealed too much. I've frightened you." He was infuriated at himself.

"I'm not afraid, Hal."

"Why were you trembling, then?" He hated the idea he might have made her fear him.

"I tremble for *you*. From . . . desire."

Oh, sweet, hesitant innocent.

What an extraordinary woman she was, so frank and open. Completely the opposite to himself. But nothing could have prepared him for what came next.

"I don't have a great deal of experience of such matters." Her voice was so quiet he had to lean in to hear her. "But the basic fact is I enjoyed my . . . *our* . . . lovemaking and was curious to attempt it again."

Dear God.

He dared not come any closer, nor attempt to touch her. If ever there was a moment when a man should be kissing a woman, this was it. But he wasn't just any man.

"We'll talk about this further," he managed. "It was heaven, but we can't simply launch into some torrid affair. There's too much to think about. I long to take you, my darling, if you're foolish enough to take *me*, but it must be done in my own way, in my own time. Now, forgive me—I must return to the folly. Shall I walk you back inside?"

Was it his imagination, or did she give a sigh of disappointment? And was she swaying slightly? He moved forward swiftly and took her by the elbows.

"Tia, what's wrong?"

"Nothing, nothing. I may have drunk too much claret with supper, that's all. I felt light-headed for a moment. It will pass."

"I'm not taking any chances." Wrapping an arm about her waist, he pulled her against his side. "I'll carry you in if need be. It's hot and sultry tonight, and perhaps you're too tightly laced. I would offer to loosen your corsets if I could trust myself to do nothing more."

"Is that so? I suppose it might be best if you didn't. Mama would wonder how I came to be unlaced."

Hal's fingers stroked the slender curve of her waist, relishing the touch of Tia's body pressed against his. "She wouldn't suspect *me*, surely? She'd come up with some purely innocent explanation."

"I doubt she'd suspect you. She still thinks of you as a distant, slightly menacing figure, with ice in his veins, not blood."

"But we both know differently, don't we?" He slid his hand down to her hip. Oh, why was he doing this to himself? It was sweet torture. He needed to escort her back into the house before his defenses crumbled, and he threw her down on the lawn to ravish her.

Without waiting for her response, he took firm hold of her shoulder and walked her rapidly through the cloisters, holding her lantern in his free hand.

The shadows swayed and diminished as the light struck them. "Are you happy to return this way? I assume it's the way you came. Don't worry. I shall watch you to ensure the demons and gargoyles don't spring to life and pounce upon you."

"Hal, I do believe you're trying to tease me. It demonstrates a considerable improvement in your state of mind."

"How thoughtful of you to point it out."

"Sarcasm, too. Why, you are becoming almost human." Tia was taunting him now. She must be recovering.

"Little witch." He swept her into in his arms, and she melted into his embrace like a wilting rose. His mouth covered hers as he succumbed to her spell, and her lips parted to welcome him, drugging him with their heady taste. Her fingers dug into the fine wool of his jacket as she clung to him, raising herself on tiptoe to increase the pressure of their kiss.

His arms wound about her waist, pressing her firmly against his body as he plundered her mouth, hungrily, inexorably. At her invitation, he thrust in his tongue to meet hers, teasingly withdrawing, then pushing in again until her jaw went slack and she surrendered all control to him.

Ah, if only this kiss could last forever. Nothing in the world was more important than two people united in desire, drinking their pleasure from each other's lips, igniting the flames in each other's bodies. The moment was timeless, boundless, completely exhilarating.

But he had to end this before it went too far. He'd fallen once. For the sake of her reputation, for the sake of their future happiness, he must *not* fall again. With a last, lingering caress of her lips, he pulled away.

He'd lifted her clear off the ground in his enthusiasm. As he released the pressure, she slid slowly down his body, creating a friction in his loins that sent prickles of excitement sparking through him. Their kiss had brought him to a potent hardness, proclaiming shamelessly how much his body wanted hers.

"I must return to the folly." Must he? His words sounded hollow, and he wondered who he was trying to convince. "Thank you, Tia."

"It was only a kiss, Hal." Her voice was husky. "No need to thank me. I wanted to do it, to be reminded of what you tasted like."

"I can't believe you've forgotten." She hadn't, surely?

"Well, your kisses are so rarely given, it's easy to forget what they're like. Almost as rare as your smile, but I hope that can be improved upon."

"Don't be angry with me, Tia. I'm trying to preserve your innocence, and my peace of mind."

"No, you're not." The change in her tone warned him she was in earnest now. What had he done to annoy her?

"You're fully unwilling to face up to the realities of a proper interaction with another person," she continued. "You do something that pricks your conscience and choose to hide in your folly rather than face the consequences."

She tried to wriggle away from him, but he tightened his grip. "I don't hide myself in there. I'm working. And thinking."

"Working at what? You have an abbey to *work* in."

He stroked her back soothingly. "This is something so personal, I'm not ready to share it."

"Not even with me?"

"I *will* share it with you, my wonderful Galatea, one day." He wouldn't find it easy, but he saw now it had to be done if he was to have any chance of happiness.

"Why not now? Don't you trust me?"

"I trust you more, I think, than I've ever trusted a woman before. I consider you my friend. But you need to trust my judgment for a change. The time isn't right for me, even if it is for you. Now, I've accepted that Polly can have her small gathering, and I've kissed you thoroughly, even though I had every intention of allowing you to escape to bed untouched. Please don't test my resolve any farther tonight, Tia. One day you will know everything. Be patient."

With that, he drew her gently to him, brushed his lips across her forehead, and strode away.

Chapter 32

Though anxious about Polly's picnic, Tia made every effort to hide the fact. This close to mid-August, the weather was too hot and horribly humid. The air had filled with flying ants, invading the house, driving the servants mad. Tia was terrified the insects would land on the muffins, or dive into the cream jug.

But these annoyances failed to eclipse the enthusiasm created in the household by the prospect of the children's picnic. Polly was so excited she was beside herself. A pity her father wasn't here to see how happy he'd made his child by softening his attitude.

All the same, the girl lacked confidence, and as soon as the first guests arrived, she hid behind Tia's skirts, crying, "Oh, Miss Wyndham, I don't know what to say to them."

"Don't be silly, child—*they* are the guests, and it's up to them to please *you*. And don't worry if you're shy, as some of them are probably shy also. How about if you all go and play catch on the lawn? There'll be little need to make conversation."

As Tia hurried past with Polly in search of a ball, Aldergate entered through the front door and stood in the entrance hall, looking important.

"Lord and Lady Fanshawe and their daughters Georgiana and Harriet," he announced.

Lord and Lady Fanshawe? Whatever were they doing here? It was the children who'd been invited, not the whole family. Heart pounding, Tia curtsied awkwardly and extended her hand. "Why, your ladyship, and sir, what a pleasure. We'd only expected the children's nannies to be with them."

It was definitely *not* a pleasure. The modest garden party hadn't been designed with the nobility in mind.

It soon became evident why the Fanshawes had accompanied their daughters. As Tia's mother joined their little group, Lady Fanshawe peered around with keen interest. "Pleased to make your acquaintance, Mrs. Wyndham, Miss Wyndham. Is Lord Ansford not at home?"

He was not. He'd rigidly refused to budge on the issue of being present at his daughter's party and had escaped to London.

Coward.

"No, my lady, he's gone up to Town on urgent business."

"A pity. We so hoped to see him again. Where would you like us to deposit ourselves? I hope you have somewhere cool, as our coach was unbearably stuffy."

Tia showed them into the morning room, fortuitously tidied the previous day. Maintaining a poise she was far from feeling, she sent for iced punch and gazed in silent horror at the aristocrats who had invaded her children's party, wondering how she was supposed to entertain them.

While the Fanshawes settled in, she whispered to Mama, "You were in charge of the invitations—you didn't invite Lord and Lady Fanshawe, did you?"

Her mother appeared troubled. "Not intentionally, no. Maybe they invited themselves as such people sometimes do. I don't think there was anything ambiguous in my wording."

Mrs. Dunne appeared in the doorway, gesturing frantically, and Tia was forced to leave Mama to make polite conversation with their august visitors while she dealt with the housekeeper.

"There's another carriage, miss! With more gentlemen, and ladies, and children. I'm almost certain one of the men is the Earl of Bedwyn."

"But this was meant to be a children's party. The food is aimed at childish tastes, not an adult palate. And we can't expect the Earl of Bedwyn to enjoy sitting outside on an upturned bucket or log."

The housekeeper must have heard the tension in her voice, for she gave her a cheerful nod. "We could bring the chairs and occasional tables out of the Great Hall and set them up in the cloister where it's cool. If some of us are detailed to take care of the adults, perhaps you, Betsy, and Nurse can deal with the children."

"Can his lordship's larder and cellars cope with these unanticipated arrivals?"

"Of course. Don't trouble yourself, miss. I'll speak to Cook and Aldergate directly. Oh, I hear another carriage, excuse me."

"Thank you, Mrs. Dunne." Thank heaven for supportive servants. Hal had chosen them well.

The housekeeper beamed as she curtsied. "It's my pleasure. Foxleaze has been silent for long enough."

Once everyone had finished arriving, there were some forty guests, where Tia had been expecting ten. There had to be a reason for this debacle, and she had a strong suspicion of where the fault lay. When one of the children proudly flapped her invitation in front of her, Tia grabbed and scanned it. She let out a heavy sigh.

Mama had worded the invitation *very* badly and was thus entirely to blame. But she was enjoying herself so much, acting the part of hostess, Tia didn't have the heart to rebuke her. All the servants—and even some of the adult visitors—had joined in to help with fetching, carrying, and supervising the children's games. Everyone was brilliantly cheerful, despite the chaos, and Tia couldn't help but be proud of what had been achieved.

Every amusement that could be conjured up was brought outside, including a harp for one young lady who offered to play, and an archery butts for whoever amongst the adults wished to demonstrate their skill. Unfortunately, the children couldn't be trusted to play croquet, as they wielded the mallets more like weapons. The adults cheerfully appropriated the game.

From snatches of overheard conversation, it was obvious the local gentry had come largely to see the reclusive Lord Ansford, the consensus that more than enough time had elapsed for him to perform his duties again, both social and legal. No one mentioned the late baroness's demise, nor the part Hal was rumored to have had in it. Tia was so relieved, she couldn't wait to tell him the good news.

Her opportunity came a good deal sooner than expected. She'd just headed back into the house to fetch a kerchief for the game of Blind Man's Bluff, when she cannoned into Hal himself, standing at the foot of the main stairwell.

Chapter 33

Pleasure washed through Tia, and she held out her hands in welcome. "Hal, how splendid. You've returned earlier than expected."

In a harsh voice that instantly wiped the joy from her heart, he growled, "What in the name of all that's holy is going on? I could barely get my carriage round to the coach house for all the horses, traveling barouches, and lackeys thronging the drive. Wasn't this meant to be a small party of children? All of whom were, in fact, supposed to have gone home a full hour ago?"

"I'm afraid everyone had friends and relations staying, so they brought them along. It would have been rude to turn anybody away. Hal—"

He thrust past her and mounted the stairs two at a time. Reaching the landing, he stared through the long window, his body rigid.

How could he turn his back on her? This wasn't her fault. She hastened after him to explain, but he spun around and pinned her with a thunderous look. "I gave permission for a small, private affair, and you have turned it into a riot. Is this how I'm to be repaid for giving you what you want? Will you forever be taking advantage of me?"

"I didn't mean—"

"Out of my way." Hal speared her with a steely gaze. "This is *my* house, and I'm going to send them all home *now*."

She shrank back, aghast. Surely not even *he* would inflict such an insult on their guests? Mama would be mortified, as would Polly. How could they bear the shame? He must be brought to see reason. She opened her mouth to protest, but the words died on her tongue.

Hal had paled, his face stonier than a statue's. His blue eyes glinted, his jaw clamped firm, clearly enraged. Before she could stop him, he cantered back down the stairs and strode toward the front door.

She ran after him and caught his elbow, but he shook her off.

"Leave me alone." His tone was dangerously soft. "I can't believe you've betrayed my trust like this. I thought so much better of you."

"Hal, no, it's all a terrible mistake," she cried, but he'd already reached the door. She followed in his wake as he marched around the side of the house toward the cloisters and caught up with him outside the archway. She grabbed the back of his coat, desperate to stop him going any farther.

"Please, don't. Polly will be so ashamed if you throw everyone out. This wasn't meant to happen, believe me." She pressed her forehead against the soft wool of his coat, squeezing her eyes tight shut, hoping he'd see reason.

The tension in his muscles eased a fraction. His body heaved with emotion, but he didn't go forward or shout at his visitors. Had she won? She peeped out to see if anyone had noticed their altercation.

The party was in full swing. The grounds were flooded with people of all ages, sitting beneath ingeniously rigged-up canopies, strolling underneath parasols, chasing balls, chasing ducks, playing croquet, and even reading. It looked as if a genteel version of Chippenham fair had come to Foxleaze—there was even a handful of children dancing to the out-of-tune notes of the harp.

To any other aristocrat, this enjoyable gathering would have been considered a triumph. To Henry Pelham, eighth Baron Ansford, it was a catastrophe.

Hoping for a last-minute reprieve, Tia stood in front of him and looked up, praying he'd see the desperation in her eyes.

He simply stared past her, ignoring the mute plea. A muscle twitched in his jaw, and his chest heaved with such indignation, she expected the buttons on his black waistcoat to fly off.

"Please Hal, *don't*." Her voice was a mere whisper.

As if coming back to her from far away, he lowered his gaze to her face, but there was no focus in his eyes. Without a word, he turned smartly on his heel and marched back the way he'd come.

She sank back against the stone pillar of the archway, like a puppet whose strings had been cut. Pressing a hand against her midriff, she waited for the panic to ebb away. Hal had quit the battlefield. But had he left her victorious or had he retreated, intending to regroup?

The only way to find out and avert potential disaster was to follow him.

Chapter 34

Hal dragged off his coat and threw it onto the bed. He'd been unutterably rude to Tia, but finding his house teeming with people, when he'd hoped to have it—and her—to himself, was intolerable.

Pushing a hand through his hair, he crossed to the window, peered out, grimaced, and strode back to the door. A few more moments' pacing failed to improve his mood, so he slumped down on the chair in his dressing room and regarded his reflection balefully in the mirror.

So, this was how he appeared when angry. Not a pleasant sight. No wonder she'd backed away from him. Even so, she'd persisted in trying to speak to him. The woman had courage, at least.

He rolled his eyes. *Oh, Tia.* She'd let him down so badly. Would it always be like this between them, with him so besotted he couldn't help but give in to her demands? After which she'd abuse any concessions he'd made, and completely betray his trust?

If only he hadn't fallen head-over-heels in love.

He wanted her, body and soul, for all eternity. But would marriage to Tia be any less painful than his marriage to Mary? Tia would spoil Polly, and he'd spoil them both by lavishing too much affection on them—and they'd unite to take advantage of him at every turn.

He'd become indulgent, as he had been with Mary—or *thought* he had been—and would pander to their every whim until they no longer respected, or even *liked* him.

Unbearable.

The spoiling of Polly could be avoided if he sent her away to school as originally planned. But it would set Tia against him, not an auspicious beginning for their married life. Was his love strong enough to weather the storms that would come? Was his love even strong enough to weather their troubles *now?*

It must be. It had to be. He'd known when he took her innocence marriage was inevitable, whether she became *enceinte* or not. He was an honorable man, despite appearances, and he'd do the right thing. Love could flourish between a wedded couple, even if the match had been arranged—or forced.

Now was the time for him to practice optimism. A solution could be found for Polly to satisfy both himself and Tia. Soon they would wed, and he'd do his damnedest to be a loving husband, a protective father. He must give as much of his newly-awakened heart as he could spare and be prepared to deal with its ill usage by his wayward, ungovernable intended.

The one thing he would *not* do was abandon her to take up his political campaigning once more. That was a mistake he'd no intention of making twice.

He gazed at his reflection again. The color had returned to his cheeks, and a beam of sunlight slanting through the window picked out the dark gold-blonde of his hair.

He raised an eyebrow at himself. He could actually be quite a handsome devil if he put his mind to it. But not wearing funereal black.

Blue and gold had been his gaudy colors of choice—not for the House, of course—and he wondered if he still had anything like that in his closet. Foolish as it seemed, he had no idea, since Symons ruled that realm.

There was a shout from outside, followed by the sound of breaking glass.

Dear God, was this horde of vandals going to destroy his house as well as his garden? Tia had a lot to answer for.

He gnawed on his lip. He owed her an apology first. It would be difficult, but if he wanted to have any kind of future with her, he must swallow his pride and relax his rules. It would also be painful, like bursting, new-born, out of a too-tight skin, but he'd do his best.

Fear clutched at his heart. What if he offered for her and she refused? This wasn't the first time he'd been hideously unpleasant to her.

He must act fast if he was to save the day. Decision made, he leapt from the chair and pulled the bell rope for his valet.

Chapter 35

Tia lingered on the half landing, with only the once-fearsome suit of armor to keep her company. Hal had been gone a long time, and she didn't know if she should go in to him, or whether it would be better to wait.

Eventually, she could bear the uncertainty no longer, so she hurried up the stairs and along to the door connecting his half of the house with the rest. Once through and into the corridor, she made her way to his suite of rooms, then hesitated.

The sound of voices reached her from behind his dressing room door. Shifting closer to listen, she could make out the clipped tones of his valet, Symons. What were they talking about? Hal had seemed too angry to want to indulge in conversation with anyone. What was going on?

She'd raised her hand to knock, when the door swung open, making her jump. Hal stood there, doing up the buttons on the front of a bright yellow waistcoat embroidered with daisies. Her jaw dropped.

He'd also donned a pair of breeches in cream silk, and now wore a jacket of pale blue, with a striped yellow lining. This colorful ensemble was topped by a cream silk cravat. Her eyes widened. Gazing past his shoulder, she caught the eye of his valet, Symons—and thought she saw him winking.

As Hal stood there in all his magnificence, gazing down at her with his bright blue eyes, she was reminded forcibly of statues of the sun god Apollo. Hal was like the god in mortal form . . . had Apollo ever dressed in modern-day clothing.

She cast around her addled brain for something to say but found nothing. Certainly, nothing that could be voiced in a servant's hearing.

Hal stepped forward, shot her a look that set fires blazing up and down her body, and strode off toward the cloister stairs. She hurried after him in total confusion, but his rapid stride soon left her behind. Why gaze at her as if he was mentally stripping her naked, then march off without a word?

She pursued him to the foot of the stairs leading into the cloisters, then hung back in the shadow of an archway as he approached the nearest group of adults. Was he going to throw them out? Had the moment she'd been dreading arrived?

Heart in mouth, she saw him greet them with a brief bow. The response was immediate—the ladies became flustered, and the gentlemen were clearly taken aback. It was barely a moment, however, before everyone seemed to be trying to talk to the master of Foxleaze at the same time.

He began a perambulation of the garden party, and Tia followed in his wake, like a faithful dog who'd been chastised and was unsure of its welcome.

The effect of Hal's presence among his guests made her think of a bear sticking its paw into a beehive. Everywhere there was an excited buzz and hum, affecting even the children. They all watched, awestruck, as the splendid owner of the abbey strode amongst them in all his finery, honoring them with the light of his smile and his compelling personality.

When Polly saw her papa and ran to fling her arms about him, Tia's eyes grew moist. But she had no time to reflect on this development, because a small child tugged on her skirt, wanting to know when Blind Man's Bluff would be starting because it was his favorite game. Much as she would have loved to trail after Hal, she had duties to perform.

Throughout the remainder of the hot August afternoon, she was kept busy supplying the children with games, cakes, and lemon cordial. Some of their parents approached and complimented her on her skills with their offspring, thanking her for hosting such a pleasurable event.

It delighted her to hear such praise, but beneath her cheerful aspect, her heart was raw. Every time she spotted Hal, he was surrounded by a throng of chattering, enthusiastic people. When he could escape such attentions, he was most likely dashing to the assistance of some young female, helping to open an awkward parasol, positioning a chair, or tuning up an instrument.

Every female in the place was as affected by his good looks and virile allure as *she* was. At least it seemed like it, from the way they simpered, dropped their reticules and handkerchiefs for him to pick up, and fluttered their eyelashes at him when he complied.

More than once, Tia seriously contemplated running off to her room to have a damned good cry. Henry Pelham, eighth Baron Ansford had, it seemed, finally been restored to Society.

But was he now lost to *her?*

Chapter 36

The weather had refused to break, resulting in an uncomfortably sultry night. Hal's thoughts were too tangled to facilitate sleep, and his guilt gnawed at him until it hurt. He tossed off the sheet and rose, crossing to the open window to see if any breeze was to be had.

Not much. Sighing, he gazed in the direction of the folly. He hadn't gone across there after supper to continue his homage to Mary—the urge remained, yes, but the compulsion had lost its power now. Besides, he'd been wearied from his trip to London, and his exertions in the afternoon.

So, in view of that weariness, why had the gods only permitted him an hour's sleep before goading him into wakefulness again?

It was Tia. Of course, it was. He couldn't exorcise the image of her shaken expression when he'd railed at her this afternoon. His behavior had been inexcusable, and he hadn't yet found the opportunity to apologize. Each time he tried to corner her, she seemed to be doing something for Polly or the other children. He began to wonder why he had servants at all if nobody bothered to use them.

Unless, of course, she was deliberately avoiding him.

He pressed against the windowsill, enjoying the cooler air on his naked flesh, but it wasn't cold enough. The only answer was a swim. It would banish any further hope of sleep, but perhaps when he came back in the chill air of the morning, he could set his thoughts straight and decide what he needed to say to Tia.

Pulling on breeches, shoes, and a shirt, he turned to appraise himself in the glass. Frowning, he recalled how grim an aspect he'd presented yesterday, with fury issuing from every pore. From now on, he must make the effort to smile a good deal more.

Particularly at Tia.

His gaze dropped to the miniature portrait of Mary, propped on the dressing table. Picking it up, he stared at it for a long time. Eventually, with a murmured apology, he opened a small drawer and placed the picture inside. A modest beginning, but better than no beginning at all.

As he lit a lantern to illuminate his walk, the flare of light seemed to burn the cares from his shoulders, offering him the promise of a better, brighter future.

A finger of moonlight grazed the path as he struck out toward the stand of trees by the river. He kept to the verge, not liking the sound of his feet on the gravel, a sound that seemed to tear the peace of the night asunder. One of the wolfhounds, Zacky, bounded up to sniff at him, and greet him. But instead of loping back to his post as he should, the dog pricked up his ears and nosed at his master, staring pointedly down the driveway.

"What, boy? Have you seen a fox?" Hal fondled one of the coarse ears and allowed his hand to be licked. The dog kept pace with him as he strode onward, its tail swinging cheerfully from side to side, but it remained alert.

Some animal must have disturbed him. If it were an intruder, Zacky would be growling with his hackles up. Hal slowed down, and peered into the darkness, but could see nothing save the shadowy shapes of a few rabbits scattering out of their path.

"It's only rabbits, Zack. Go home now boy, home." He pointed, and gave the dog's rump a shove, prompting the animal to wag its tail even more before bounding off.

Cautiously, Hal sought the shadow of the lime trees, making sure to keep any noise to a minimum. But when he came to his bathing place, he discovered it already occupied.

Tia stood there, ankle deep in the water, her thin cotton nightgown pulled up to her knees.

Paddling? Tia was *paddling*? At first, he was annoyed she should be out in the darkness all by herself, particularly dressed only in a nightgown. But he'd promised himself not to be angry with her anymore. Besides, the dogs knew her and would protect her from any danger. A mild rebuke for making herself vulnerable must suffice.

It was abundantly clear she had no idea he was there because the next moment she grasped the hem of her nightgown and dragged it over her head.

He stood spellbound, feasting his hungry gaze on her shapely legs, her delightful pear-shaped buttocks and slender waist, and the graceful curves of her shoulders. She twisted to throw the garment on the bank behind her, treating him to a glimpse of her firm, ripe breasts with their rosy nipples— before she saw him.

With a shriek of surprise, she covered herself with her hands and splashed noisily into a deeper spot, submerging until only her head was showing. He winced on her behalf— the water there was cold, and she hadn't given herself time to get accustomed to it. It was imperative she exit immediately and get dry.

"Tia," he called softly, as he walked to the bank. "Come out before you catch a chill. No, don't frown at me—it's merely advice, not an order."

"I'm not frowning. How can you see in the darkness anyway?"

He could see quite well at night—he was used to it. But for now, for the sake of her dignity, he'd pretend he couldn't. "I assumed you would be. You can't be happy that I came upon you so unexpectedly."

"Were you watching me? How long have you been there?"

"I wasn't watching you. I've only recently arrived—I wanted a swim as it was too hot to sleep. I presume it's what you were thinking too. Or did you plan to dance naked in the woods like a maenad?"

"I don't like being spied on. Now turn your back so I can come out and dress."

"I suppose I could. But while you're a captive audience, there are a couple of things I'd like to say to you."

"Can't they wait until daylight, when I'm properly garbed and comfortable?"

Preferably not. This was far more entertaining. "I think my words will have more impact *now*. First, I want to apologize for being such a brute. I will never behave like that again."

"And if I choose not to forgive you?"

He stooped and gathered up her nightgown. It was still warm, imbued with her delightfully feminine, lavender scent. He flung it onto his shoulder. "I can choose to withhold this."

She gasped in outrage, bringing a grin to his face. "You want to play games, Hal?"

"Oh, very much. It would make you blush if you knew how much."

There was a pause. "I'll consider forgiving you if you put my nightgown within easy reach of the shore and turn your back while I get out."

"Agreed. In part." He laid the garment on the riverbank, a foot clear of the water. Then he crouched, gazing at her where she lurked in the moon-rippled water, her hair streaming about her in tantalizing swirls.

"Please take yourself further away."

He grinned back at her. "I will, but you must promise me something in return."

She eyed him with suspicion. "What must I promise?"

He said simply, "To marry me."

Chapter 37

There was a great wallowing sound from the river. Panic clutched at him—had Tia lost her footing? He was already kicking off his shoes when she emerged again, steadied herself and spluttered, "I think I must have water in my ears. What did you say?"

His shoulders relaxed. "I asked you to marry me."

A long silence ensued while the darkness seemed to close in on him, as if eager to hear the rapid beating of his heart. A thin sheen of sweat broke out on his brow, owing nothing to the heat.

She was going to refuse him. And who could blame her? What kind of heartless rogue caught a woman off-guard and used veiled threats to persuade her into marriage?

He needed different words, different deeds. Hal began to disrobe.

"What are you doing?" There was alarm in her voice.

"I'm taking off my clothes."

"For heaven's sake, why?"

He chuckled. "I don't want them getting wet when I come in to fetch you."

She sank farther until the water came to her chin. "I don't need fetching."

"You're going to come out on your own?" He pulled off his shirt.

"I might."

"*Might* isn't good enough. Now you can look away if you want to, but my breeches are coming off, too."

She didn't look away. He grinned broadly, hoping he didn't appear too lecherous, enjoying himself more than he had in years. Her eyes never left him as he waded out to join her, and most of the time—if not all—they remained above the level of his chest.

The cold water washed over his skin, making him catch his breath, as delicious shivers rippled across his belly and buttocks. "Tia, I'm in deadly earnest."

"About marriage, or about me coming out?"

"About both. I desire you above anything. I could learn to be happy again if you would allow me to become your husband—as well as your friend."

"This is all rather sudden."

He waded closer. "No, it isn't. You know how much I want you. Now, will you give me your answer before we both freeze to death?"

"Am I not allowed some time to think about it? This declaration is a bolt out of the blue."

He shook his head. Ah. Her teeth were chattering. Rapid action was required. Lifting her chilled body into his arms, he cradled her against his chest. Water flowed from her luscious curves, sending sensual rivulets down his belly and thighs as he strode back to the shallows.

His manhood swelled in response.

Businesslike, he set her down, holding her with one hand as he gave her his shirt with the other. "Dry yourself."

When she gave no sign of taking it, he rasped, "Do it, or I'll do it for you."

Grumbling, she seized it from him and turned her back.

With a shrug of resignation, he pulled on his breeches, knowing they would be soaked through in moments. Well, if it dampened his burgeoning ardor, it would be no bad thing.

Once his shoes were back on, he peered past his shoulder to see if Tia had finished drying herself.

She hadn't moved. She was staring at him. Had she been silently observing him all this time? He must look ridiculous, with no shirt on, no stockings, and breeches that stuck to him like a second skin, with a rampant hardness distorting the front of them in a way she was hardly likely to miss.

"Tia, I'm sorry."

She dropped his shirt. Her hands fell away from her body.

He swallowed painfully, once. Twice. "Tia—"

"You dry me." Her voice was an inviting purr. "Afterward, I'll dry you."

Slowly he picked up the shirt, then feasted his eyes on her moon-slick nakedness. The urge to run his hands and his lips over every single inch of her was overpowering. She was well-named Galatea, for every line, curve, shadow, dip and mound of her body was absolute perfection. She could have been the model for Pygmalion's statue, a breath of ecstasy captured in marble. The gods had truly blessed him tonight, but he was far from worthy of such a gift.

It took every ounce of his self-control, but he did as she wished and started rubbing the shirt briskly across her enticing curves, making sure his fingers never made direct contact.

She moaned softly as he worked across her buttocks and when he came to her rosy-peaked breasts, she reached for him, gripping him hard by the shoulders.

The need to take each peaked nipple in his mouth was so strong, he was dazed and shaken by his efforts to resist.

No. He wasn't going to tumble her on the ground like some love-crazed country boy but do the thing properly in the comfort of his bed, with plenty of time at their disposal and no fear of discovery.

He stood back, trying to ignore the painfully throbbing demands of his manhood. "Lift your arms," he ordered roughly. As soon as she did so, he slipped her nightgown on. Now she was decently covered, he hoped to give his violently aroused body a moment's respite.

"Let's go inside. We have much to talk about. You haven't given me your answer yet, and I want to be sure you give the correct one."

"And how will you persuade me to do that, pray?"

"You'll see. You'll see." He swept her up in his arms and carried her toward the house and the welcoming softness of his bed.

Chapter 38

Tia marveled at Hal's strength. She reveled in the shifting muscle of his bare shoulder, while her body sensed the power in every stride, in every breath.

He wanted to marry her. This wasn't the result she'd expected when she set out to reform him. He was a stranger to her in many ways, but that could be remedied in time. Wouldn't Mama be shocked? Lucy wouldn't be, of course— Tia was certain all the queries about Hal in her letters to the Duchess of Finchingfield must have given her away.

But what about Polly? What would *she* think of the prospect of having a new parent?

That could be dealt with later—there was plenty of time for a long engagement, during which they could all grow accustomed to the idea. She and Mama would probably have to live elsewhere for a while of course, as it wasn't exactly seemly for a gentleman to dwell under the same roof as his betrothed.

But her mind was leaping ahead of the facts. She hadn't accepted him.

Yet.

His arms closed tightly, protectively around her, and she buried her face against the sturdy column of his neck, where she could smell the bitter scent of his cologne mixed with the sweet musk of his skin. When she tested her lips against his flesh, the movement in his jaw told her he was smiling. She dropped a trail of kisses up to his ear, surrendering to an overwhelming urge to bite his lobe.

"Ouch! What was that for?"

"I'm sorry. I couldn't resist."

"Be more gentle next time, if you please. I may be a man, but some parts of my anatomy are equally as sensitive as yours."

She nuzzled him below the chin, kissed his jawline, the high aristocratic lines of his cheek and his temple, and the corner of his eyebrow. His eyes crinkled as he beamed again, twisting his head to return her kiss.

It proved to be quite difficult to do this and walk at the same time. Their teeth and noses clashed, sending her into giggles and him into light chuckling. A great glow of joy spread through her.

Hal was grinning, laughing. Perhaps he was even in love? She hoped as much, though he ought to damn well hurry up and tell her so.

"Put me down," she advised. "You must kiss me properly."

"Wait, we're nearly there." He set her down beneath the archway. "Deuce take it!"

"What is it?"

"Shh, my sweet. It's gone two in the morning—we don't want to awaken any of the servants, or they'll be out of sorts all day."

"You're the last person to object to someone being short-tempered, especially after yesterday."

"Hush now. I'm a reformed man. Or will be if you consent to be my wife. Have you an answer for me yet?"

"I asked for time. I meant more than ten minutes. Now, what were you cursing about?"

"We left the lantern and my shirt down by the willow tree."

"I'm sure one of the gardeners will return them."

"Yes, but what will they make of it? I don't want there to be any gossip."

She sighed. Surely, he was inured to gossip by now? "They'll simply assume you drank too much punch yesterday afternoon and forgot them after your habitual swim. They must know you swim?"

"I sincerely hope not. I keep it to myself and often go in naked. But only after dark."

She shivered deliciously at the memory of his body, slick with water in the moonlight. It would be nice to think she was the only person who had ever seen him thus.

"Come." The one simple word, uttered softly, made her spine tingle with anticipation.

"Where are we going?"

"To my dressing room, to dry off. I fear I've soaked your nightgown."

Had he? She hadn't noticed, aware only of the searing heat emanating from his naked torso.

Her skin burned in the places his hands had touched. She gulped.

"After you." He stood back to let her past him into the cloisters, and she enjoyed the image of a half-naked peer of the realm bowing politely to her. Her feet seemed to have no weight as she glided along the passageway with him at her side, and even though they hadn't a lamp, the shadows no longer menaced her.

Soon she was in the dressing room, settled in Hal's chair, every nerve alive with excitement.

He reached for a towel and applied it to the still-dripping ends of her hair. Once satisfied, he ran his fingers through it, deftly removing the tangles, but occasionally becoming distracted and placing kisses on the side of her face, her neck, and the top of her head.

Avidly, she watched his reflection in the glass, loving the way the lamplight in the room sent shadows rippling like silk across the smoothness of his shoulders and the mounded muscles of his chest. She longed to turn around and bury her face there, taste his skin, luxuriate in the sensation of the light down of hair rubbing against her cheek. But that would be too wanton.

Wouldn't it?

Once order had been restored to her hair, he gave her neck further attention. First, he applied his lips to the task, then his teeth, creating a languid desire in her limbs. When he gently bit her earlobe and tugged on it, she knew him to be a master of the art. His hot tongue dipped in and out, sending a delicious shiver chasing across her skin.

She tilted her head back, hoping for a kiss, but instead, he took advantage of her exposed neckline and delved brazenly.

Her body jerked as his warm hand took the weight of her breast, but the cloth was stretched too tightly for much activity. Hoping he wouldn't be too shocked, but desperate to give him full access to her now-aching breasts, she asked huskily, "Shall I help, my lord?"

"Mmm?" He nuzzled a roughened cheek against her temple.

"I said, can I—oh, never mind." She applied her fingers to the row of tiny buttons at the front of her nightgown and soon had them undone. This admitted his other hand, and she discovered the exquisite pleasure of having both breasts stroked at once, while her neck and shoulder continued to be nibbled and kissed.

He caught her rigid nipples between his fingers and started rubbing the tips with his thumbs. The merciless friction had her gasping for breath and craning back to expose her bosom more fully to his expertise.

Blessedly, his mouth found hers, offering reassurance that her actions, her emotions, were acceptable to him. An arrow of intense pleasure darted straight to the tiny nub of flesh between her legs, and she squeezed them together, desperate to increase the sensation.

Hal groaned against her mouth and slid his hands lower until her gown creaked at the seams.

"I think this needs to come off," she whispered as soon as his lips released her.

"Shameless hussy. You are, however, correct, but we can't do it while you're sitting down, can we?"

The next thing she knew, she was in his arms, being carried through to his bedchamber—again—and being laid down on his bed—again. Was he going to make love to her once more?

I can think of no reason for him not to.

Chapter 39

Tia sank her body blissfully into the clean, citrus smell of Hal's cologne on the pillow, mingled with the scent of lavender from the sheet. Sitting up, she eagerly pulled her nightgown over her head—and gazed at Hal.

He stood by the bed, watching her, unbuttoning his breeches. Her breath caught as his splendidly engorged member sprang free. This was what *she* had done to him—she had reduced this man with his power, his wealth, and his glorious body to this intense state of desire. His world was focused entirely on her, as was her own on him.

"Are we going to make love?" She nodded coyly at his magnificent hardness.

He tilted his head at her. "Without the benefit of wedlock? No, my dear. I gave in to temptation once and am ashamed of my lack of self-control. But it doesn't mean we can't share the pleasures of the flesh. Though you must trust me, and not be embarrassed or ashamed."

"Do I appear ashamed?" She stretched her naked limbs out across the bed.

He threw his head back and laughed. Her heart leapt. Such a revelation to hear him laugh so naturally, so easily, no longer sounding as if he tried using muscles that had forgotten how to work. She shifted across the bed as he reclined on his side. The heated tip of his manhood pressed against her leg. It was fascinating how the thing seemed to have a life of its own.

Thrills of arousal washed through her as he cradled her close, skin to skin, rocking gently against her in a taunting, tempting rhythm. When he kissed her, deeply probing her mouth with his tongue, she wound her arms around his neck and pushed her fingers into his golden hair.

Supporting himself on one elbow, his free hand busied itself with long, lavish strokes of her breasts, her belly, her hips. Her skin leapt to exquisite awareness at his touch, and she reached out, mimicking his actions, delighting in the softness of his flesh and the hardness of the muscle beneath.

She traced the pattern of downy hair adorning his torso, following the valley between the muscles of his midriff. Her fingers joined with the tantalizing forest of curls whence his manhood sprung, pressing urgently against her thigh.

Each time she tentatively explored him, he responded with a sigh, a movement, a more ardent pressure in their kiss. He repaid her by trailing a line of kisses across her collarbone before—*oh, glory*—taking one aching nipple into his mouth.

Her body arched as his tongue slid across the tender tip, bucking when his teeth first grazed, then gently nibbled at it. She rained kisses on the top of his head because it was all she could reach.

So lost was she in a sensuous daze, she barely noticed when he parted her legs. But when his finger slipped between the now-slick folds at the core of her femininity, something seemed to burst inside her, and she clutched at him, moaning.

Gradually, the expert stroking of his finger brought her body to a state of excitement so intense she knew not how to bear it, and she rocked her hips up, down, craving release.

Would he penetrate her again? Unite his potent masculinity with her soft femininity, fill her with his essence, become one with her?

Through the miasma of pleasure, there was a pull of disappointment. He'd told her he wouldn't enter her again until they were married. How could she possibly wait?

"Please," she begged against his mouth, reaching for him.

"I won't take you now. But touch me, Tia, please. Don't be afraid. I need to find release."

He pulled her hand down to his throbbing member, and she gripped it firmly, eliciting a low groan from deep in his throat. Fascinated, she ran her fingers along the hot, hard shaft, tested its weight, explored the skin, softer and finer than anything she had ever touched—and his body arched and bucked as hers had.

His fingers slid deep inside her, massaging her intimately, his palm pressing against her mound—and she lost all control. Time and place shifted to nothing but her body and his, clenched together in intense concentration, eking out each drop of sinful sensation, beyond words, beyond thought.

Anxious to savor every last instant of pleasure, she squeezed her legs tight and continued to run her hand firmly up and down his shaft, stroking, delighting in the way it made him groan and squirm, as lost in the moment as she, both of them devoted slaves to the earthly delights of the flesh.

His breathing quickened, his body tightened, and his hand came up to grasp her shoulder. With a cry, he relaxed against her, chest heaving, spasms rippling across his body.

The grip on her shoulder eased, and he nuzzled into her neck like a child. She wrapped a leg around him, bringing him as close into her embrace as she could. They were now so hot she half expected to see steam coming off their bodies, but she couldn't bear to let go of him, to release her hold on the man who had brought her such fulfillment.

When his breathing finally returned to normal, he shifted and lay on his back, pulling her head onto the pad of his shoulder. A sticky coldness against her leg verified he'd spilled his essence. Next time, when they were married, he would be inside her and his seed would not be wasted.

Her thoughts gradually came back into focus. There was, of course, only one answer to the question he had asked earlier. There was only one result to truly satisfy them both.

But dared she give that answer when there was so much she didn't yet know about him?

Chapter 40

So, this is happiness.

Pleasantly sated, Hal curled his body around the woman he loved, enjoying the gentle rhythm of her breathing. He couldn't wipe the grin off his face.

Tia shifted slightly. "About the question you asked me earlier."

He loved the way her voice reverberated through him. "Yes?" Suddenly alert, his heartbeat sped up. He actually forgot to inhale.

"Well, the answer is yes, Mr. Henry Pelham, Lord Ansford. I *will* marry you."

Joy ignited a blaze of light in his heart, banishing the darkness. He held her tightly, hoping she would sense the love in him—as well as the insatiable need—and to his delight, she turned in his embrace and pressed kisses on his brow, his mouth, and his eyelids.

He drew his lips slowly across hers, his breathing soft, scarce daring to believe he'd won her. "You've saved my soul, Tia. You've made a man of me once more, and I intend to make you proud of your creation."

"I'm already proud of you, Hal. I love you, truly, despite your faults. Maybe even because of them."

He let her tease him, too ecstatic to complain. Leaning upon his elbow, he gazed down at her. "I don't deserve it of course, but I'll do everything in my power to make you happy."

"Even to the extent of changing your mind about Polly?"

He considered this for a moment. "In the interests of maintaining the peace, I concede Polly doesn't have to be sent away. So long as you don't spoil her too much. When she reaches her eleventh birthday, she can choose what school she wants to attend. I promise not to press her to go to Miss Gates's."

"Hal, you don't know how thrilled that makes me."

"That's good to hear."

"Not that I wasn't happy already after . . . after what you did to me."

He raised his eyebrows. "Indeed? I'm delighted to have discovered such latent passion in you."

She looked down the length of his body, and he sprang to life again at her sensuous appraisal. "And *I* am delighted to have discovered such *patent* passion in you."

"Ah yes, the eternal optimism of the male genitalia. My little man assumes we can't be satisfied with a single encounter and is now ready for the next."

"So why keep him waiting?"

"Temptress. I'm surprised at you, Tia. I can see you really putting me to work."

Grinning like a cat that had got at the cream, she stroked a hand across his chest before snagging it in the chain he wore around his neck.

The key to the folly. He could tell from her expression its secret stood like a gulf between them, reminding him there was a lot yet to be shared, and a great deal he needed her to comprehend.

"Hal, the folly—"

He wrapped his fingers around hers. "I know, my love. There must be no secrets between us now. Tomorrow you shall see the project on which I've been working. I hope, I pray, it will make no difference to what we have. For what we've found is precious, Tia, so rare, some people never find it in their entire lives."

She frowned. "You're frightening me. Is there something in there to make me stop loving you?"

"I sincerely hope not. I don't know what I'd do if you changed your mind." He didn't even want to consider the possibility. Not now. Not *ever*.

"When shall we go? At first light?"

"You don't trust me not to rush in there before you come, and hide anything that might be offensive to you?" He was only half-joking.

"I should trust you, shouldn't I? If I didn't, I should never have given you the means to ruin my reputation."

"You are equally as capable of ruining me. Don't abandon your creation now, or I'll become a fearsome beast like Frankenstein's monster, and you'll have to bear the guilt for the rest of your life."

Tia gazed up at the silken canopy above his bed and let out a sigh. "Can't you explain now what's in there? Does it have something to do with your late wife?"

"It has everything to do with her. She used to enjoy the tower and the wonderful views it gave. Before Polly was born, we often went up there for a picnic on the roof, though the jackdaws usually had more of our food than we did."

The memory was fading, as if a veil had been drawn across. It saddened him.

"Are you still in love with her?"

Only in the remotest corner of his heart. It was complicated, though. In time, Tia would understand. "How can I be, when I have you? There's no comparison between the real, living thing, and a ghost. Don't ever doubt the strength of my affection, Tia. I'm a man of strong convictions."

"If I'm to take her place, you must promise if anything bad happens to me, you won't carry the burden of guilt and grief for so many years."

He gazed into her ardent, beautiful face, and gathered her to him, pressing her close to his heart. Perhaps now would be a good moment to unleash the spirit that had been haunting him. If he told Tia the whole, sordid story of the latter part of his marriage, he would be cleansed, relieved. At least that way, she would know what risks she took in agreeing to marry him.

"Tia, I have something to tell you that must go no further than this room."

She nodded her head solemnly.

Taking a deep breath, he nestled his head on her breast. And told her everything.

Chapter 41

Tia had stayed with Hal until the sun rose, her heart bleeding for him as he had revealed his tale, and she did all she could to offer comfort. Again and again, she'd told him how much she loved him, and reassured him he was worthy of every sliver of her love, worthy of every last drop of her heart's blood.

Recalling his memories had caused him such pain, she'd feared he would weep. But he was strong—perhaps even more so than he realized. He'd told her how much he admired her for surviving deprivation and loss without becoming hard and bitter, as he had.

He had praised her compassion and patience until she'd begged him to stop, lest her head explode with pride. And he'd made her promise never to let any resentment simmer, but to always tell him if he let her down in any way. It was an easy promise to make, and she had insisted on his word that he would do the same.

After a parting she had great difficulty in making, she'd returned to her room and strove to give the impression of having been there all night.

When she went down to breakfast, Hal was there, making the meal into exquisite torture.

To have him so close and yet so far, to receive the knowing, smoldering glances from his blue eyes and not be able to respond to them, was hell on earth. She could hardly believe Mama didn't notice the atmosphere between them— it was charged like a thunderstorm. Tia tasted not one single bite, for her hunger lay in only one direction.

Both she and Hal had agreed to a brief engagement. He planned to obtain a special license today, after a declaration, in the cool gray hours before dawn, of no wish to be separated from her any longer than need be.

It had also been agreed to make the announcement tonight, at dinner. Polly was to come down from the nursery, and Hal would join them all in the dining room, dressed in his best. He would present Tia with his late mother's pearl and ruby ring as a token of his intent and after that—hopefully— the happy couple would receive the approval of their nearest and dearest.

As soon as breakfast was done, Tia made her excuses to Polly and left her in the care of Nurse before hurrying down to meet Hal. He joined her with an expression of delight that warmed her to her very soul.

Despite his smile, when she took his arm, a tremor ran through him. Why? Was he worried she'd disapprove, that she'd be wounded by what she saw within the folly? Surely, their love was strong enough to overcome this last obstacle?

When they reached the top of the folly steps, he lifted her hand and kissed each fingertip, before removing the key from around his neck, and inserting it into the lock.

She took a deep breath and entered the gloomy tower. He busied himself around her, lighting lanterns and candles, sending the shadows flying against the walls. The chamber they were in was smaller than she expected, overwhelmed by the number of drawings and sketches plastering the walls. A great swathed object in the middle of the floor took up space as well, its shape obscured by a stiff, paint-spattered canvas.

She glanced around her again and saw a workbench loaded with tools—hammers, chisels, mauls, all covered in fine white dust. There was grit on the floor too, gray like the mortar but paler where it had blended with the white.

Puzzled, she approached the canvas to draw it aside, but Hal seized hold of her wrist.

"Not yet, my love. I want to show you upstairs first."

Making her way carefully up the gritty stairs, she found herself in another circular chamber. This one smelled of turpentine. Several easels bearing covered canvases were set about the edges of the room.

On a small table in the middle stood a set of paint pots, brushes, and stoneware vessels. Pegs driven into the walls held several aprons, all speckled with paint.

An artist's studio. Hal was a painter.

"You're an artist? *This* is your wicked secret?" The sense of relief was so powerful she almost swooned. She'd been worrying herself to death about this?

"Wait." He lifted the cloth from one of the canvases and held up a lamp for her to see.

She stared at a half-finished picture of a woman holding a book, her dress a dark blur of eager brushstrokes. But she recognized the dress—her favorite, the one with the stripes.

The face. *Her* face.

He was painting a portrait of her, from memory. She leaned in close enough to see the brushstrokes, individual blobs of white making the light shine out of dark eyes, the carefully placed streaks of darker red that gave shape to lips.

My lips.

Hal hovered behind her, waiting. But when she reached out to stroke a finger across the shiny surface, he caught at her hand. "Careful. It may not be quite dry. If you press on it, it'll smudge."

An unspoken question hung between them. Eventually, she said, "You have quite a talent." She heard his exhalation of breath and knew her opinion mattered to him a great deal. But what were all the other canvases? With a queasy tension in her gut, she approached another easel and lifted the cloth.

This portrait was complete. It showed a slender woman in a yellow dress, with guinea-gold curls framing a perfectly oval face, and blue-gray eyes staring out at the observer, bearing an expression of detached hauteur. Beautiful, but proud—that was how the artist had captured the woman Tia now recognized as the late baroness.

There were other pictures—on the walls, on the table, pinned to the back of the door. Some were pastel, some charcoal; a few were watercolors . . . but they were all of the same woman.

Hal's late wife.

Tia's scalp tingled as a sense of dread settled on her. Seizing Hal's lantern, she returned to the room below and stood once more, staring at the covered shape on the floor. With a flourish, she whipped the cloth away and cast it aside.

And froze in amazement.

There, stretched out on a roughly hewn bed of marble, lay a perfect representation of a woman. Her hands were folded across her breasts and her hair, carved in elaborate detail, spilled across a pillow of gray-veined stone.

The sight stole Tia's breath. Stunned, she forced her legs to move and bent low over the dead face, examining the sculptor's art. The contours were there, the full lips, the deep eyelids, even delicate scratches for the lashes brushing against carved cheeks.

A perfect Venus in death, a monument to lost beauty.

But more incredible than the depiction of the woman was the veil draping her face. A veil of marble which interrupted her perfect features in folds like those of the finest lawn cloth.

Tia turned to Hal. "You? *You* did this?"

"For my sins, yes. I have worked on it nearly every day since her death, as a monument to her."

"Hal, it's . . . it's truly remarkable." Tears burned her eyes. What else could she say? Here, forever enshrined in stone, was a sculpted masterpiece, testament to a man's love for his lost wife, a symbol of his devotion.

How was she ever to compete with this deceased paragon of beauty? How could she ever hope to take Mary's place in his heart? Her eyes were wet with tears, her lungs so heavy she could barely breathe.

She wasn't sure if she wanted to.

"You love her even now." Her voice cracked.

"No. Tia, please, I've put it all behind me. Now, I have you. How can I love a ghost, an idea, a memory? Not when I have found a living, breathing, beautiful woman who has helped me face up to—and overcome—my demons."

Oh, how she wished she could believe him. "You come here regularly," she choked out, "to commune with Mary and ask her shade for forgiveness."

"I do not. I come now to draw you, to paint *you.* See, this table is full of sketches." He gathered up a sheaf of them and thrust them at her. "See? All you."

She turned squarely to face him, wracked with sobs. "I don't believe you can love like a normal man, Hal. This work shows obsession to the point of madness."

She swallowed hard and forced out the words that tore her apart.

"I can't marry you."

Chapter 42

Hal's face paled as his eyes bore into Tia's. "Don't say that. Don't tell me I'm a madman. I'm an artist. I've been striving for perfection, creating a masterpiece. It's what artists do."

All she could think about was the fact he'd closeted himself away from the world for three years, building a shrine to his dead wife. She fought down the bile rising in her throat.

"I can't do this. I can't. I can never match up to her."

"Darling, I care nothing for her now, nothing. I'll have all the sketches, all the pictures, taken out and burned— whatever you wish. It is only *you* who has been able to bring the light back into my life. I need you to trust me. When it comes to Mary, there is no competition, I swear it. Don't throw away our chance of happiness. Tell me how I might prove my love to you, and I will."

But she was no longer listening. Her heart had shattered into a thousand tiny fragments, glass-sharp splinters that pricked and stung, goading her for being such a fool as to fall in love with a man obsessed with the memory of his dead wife. His charismatic, stunningly beautiful wife. Whom he'd loved to the end, even though she had cuckolded him and condemned him to do penance for the rest of his life by committing suicide right in front of him.

Turning her back on Hal, Tia made for the outside door.

She thought she heard him call after her to take care, but her body hardly knew what it did. All she knew was the need to quit this dreadful place, hie away from the tomb of all her hopes and into the sunlight and fresh air.

The walls of the folly seemed to shudder and close in around her, and when she burst out through the door, the stairs bucked beneath her as if they were alive. She struggled to find her way down, her eyes blurred with tears, limbs shaking in abject misery.

The rock under her feet gave an abrupt shudder, and she lurched forward several steps before she was able to regain her balance. She reached the level surface of the lawn and heard Hal call out to her.

But he wasn't begging her to return to him. He was shouting, "Run, Tia, run!"

Catching the note of fear in his voice, she turned back and saw him swaying at the top of the stairway while the whole mountain of stone rocked beneath him. Unable to tear her eyes from the terrifying spectacle, she froze, torn between rushing back to help and keeping herself out of danger.

White-faced and furious, he yelled again, waving her away. She stumbled backward as the ground shook. With an almighty roar, the tower and its base blurred, expanded, then shivered into pieces. She threw herself down as dust and shards of rock billowed toward her, slicing into her skin, embedding themselves in her hair.

A sound, like thunder, rolled off into the distance. Moments later the ground ceased to vibrate. All she could hear was the cracking, splintering sound of broken pieces of rock settling and boulders coming to rest on the grass.

Coughing and sputtering, she dragged herself onto all fours, crawling in the direction of the folly. Nothing remained of it but a jumble of black, formless rock.

Of Hal, there was no trace.

Chapter 43

Horrified, Tia stood on shaky legs, then lurched forward through the dust and rubble, casting about for any sign of Hal's bottle-green jacket.

"Hal! Hal!"

No answer. She screamed for help, hoping one of the gardeners was within earshot. In response to her shout, the sharp-eared dogs started baying. Someone from the house *must* soon realize something was wrong.

She tripped once and fell, bruising herself badly on some broken masonry, adding to the rents in her skirt and the bloody scratches on her hands. But there was no pain, only terror. Where *was* he?

A piece of dusty cloth poked out from a pile of boulders. Frantically she pushed them aside and dragged at it, but it came away in her hand, along with a splintered wooden frame. When she peered into the gap she'd created, a dead face leered back at her and she let out a horrified shriek.

The image swung into focus. Not Hal, but the veiled face of Mary's marble statue, damaged by a multitude of cracks.

Her heart pounded painfully, and she gulped in several breaths, willing herself not to faint. She must continue searching—every second counted. Her blood beat so loudly in her ears she could barely hear, but she yelled again for Hal, then stilled to listen for any response.

Suddenly, a few yards away, the rubble began to shift and slide. She scrambled across to the spot and threw herself into the task of scraping, dragging, and rolling the stones away. Something shifted underneath, dusty but animate, pushing its way back to the surface.

Hal.

"Oh, thank God you're alive." But he was a dreadful sight, his clothing torn, his pale face gray with dust, his eyes shocked and unseeing.

"Are you hurt? But you must be—your poor head." She choked down her panic—she must be strong for him now, stronger than she'd ever been.

Blood gushed from his temple, staining his battered shirt front, and he was coughing so hard as he dragged himself upright, she feared he would suffocate on the spot.

She rolled away more rubble, trying to clear a space around him so he could sit in comfort. He drew a hand across his mouth and uttered a hoarse, unintelligible sound.

"No, don't try to speak. Save your breath." She stood and screamed, "Help! Help us, somebody!"

Hal broke into another violent fit of coughing, so she knelt again and banged on his back to ease the spasm. It gave him enough relief to try extricating himself from the shattered masonry that covered his legs, but he could only move slowly, like a man emerging from water.

Tia clutched at his shoulders, blew dust from his hair, pressed her handkerchief against his flowing wound, and murmured words of comfort in his ear.

His head swiveled around, his pallid eyes roving over her body, her anxious face. "Tia, you're hurt." His voice was a painful croak. "Go and get your cuts seen to."

"Not so badly as you. Hal, you look an absolute fright."

"I don't feel too well, I confess."

"I think I hear running feet. Help is coming." *Thank heaven.*

He took her hand, brought it to his bloodied lips, and kissed her fingers as he met her eyes, though he was struggling to focus. He murmured, "It seems I have become a victim of my own folly."

Then he fainted.

The gardener's boy ran up as Tia fought not to lose consciousness herself. "Quick, get to the house and send two strong men down here with a door or a tabletop. Lord Ansford needs a stretcher. Send the fastest footman for a doctor—no, send a groom on the fastest horse. Tell Lynch, tell Symons, tell everyone."

She had no idea if her commands made any sense, but if they didn't, surely one of the people she'd sent for would be able to take charge.

Nausea and confusion threatened to consume her as she settled next to Hal, who remained unconscious. Tia cradled his head gently in her lap, making it easier to staunch the bleeding.

He mustn't die, please God, he mustn't die. There was so much she needed to say to him. There was so much they needed to share.

The discovery of the sculpted memorial had unsettled her horribly, but she'd have grown used to the idea in time, wouldn't she? And what he'd told her about artists was probably correct. After all, she had no experience to inform her judgment. She'd known long before they met, he was obsessed with his first wife, so why should she be so upset to discover he'd sculpted the late Lady Mary?

Hal was clearly a man of varied and exceptional talents. And there was no reason for her not to respect the fact.

When Tia examined her heart, she found her reason for reacting so negatively was jealousy. How foolish of her, to be jealous of a memory. The late Baroness Ansford had nothing to give her husband. But she, Miss Galatea Wyndham, had a whole lifetime of loving to offer him.

She brushed her free hand across Hal's hair, attempting to extract some of the larger slivers of rock to keep them from digging in and cutting him. His breathing was very ragged, but his eyelids were moving. He must be coming out of his swoon, giving her reason to hope.

He was a strong, healthy man—he would recover. He simply *had* to. For how else could she tell him she'd been a complete idiot to upset herself so about his sculpture? How could she show him how much she loved him and wanted to be his wife?

Right there, she swore she'd never leave him, however broken he might be, however badly injured.

She simply couldn't do without him.

Chapter 44

The events following Hal's collapse passed in a sickening blur. Tia remembered seeing his limp form borne away on a large wooden board, her handkerchief pressed against his gushing head wound. She recalled Symons helping her off the ground and carrying her back to the house, to the anxious ministrations of Mama.

She was taken into a room she'd never seen before and handed a large china basin into which she was promptly sick. There were vague memories of being bathed and dressed in a clean nightgown before being put to bed. But she didn't become fully aware again until someone dabbed a stinging liquid on her hands.

"Ouch!"

"Oh, my darling girl." Mama's voice. "Please don't fidget. Bessie is putting some alum water on your cuts. How do you feel?"

Tia tried to sit up, but the room swam. Easing back against her pillows, she waited for her mother's face to come back into focus.

"I'm nauseous and slightly dizzy. But I'm not hurt. How's Hal?"

"Somewhat damaged, but he'll recover, given time and rest. So the doctor says."

"Oh, thank heaven." Tia closed her eyes in relief. Whatever the future held, whatever happened between them, she would at least have the chance to assure Hal of her love. Had he died, thinking she hated him . . . she couldn't have lived with the guilt.

Opening her eyes again, she took in the elaborate hangings of the bed, the delicacy of the furnishings, and the tastefulness of the decoration. "What room is this?"

"The baroness's bedchamber, adjoining Ansford's suite. It's easier for the doctor if you're close together."

"Can I see Hal?" Mama had said he was alive but damaged. What did that mean, exactly?

Mama pursed her lips. "Out of the question. He's to be disturbed as little as possible. He looked so dreadful when they brought him in, I thought he was done for."

"Where's Polly?" What would it do to the girl to lose her father as well as her mother?

"In her room with Nurse, being comforted."

"Can I see her?"

"Perhaps she could be brought to see you later, but for now, you're in no fit state. Let me brush that awful grit out of your hair while Bessie finishes cleaning your cuts. I don't know what you were doing with your hands. You've broken every single nail, some of them quite badly."

"I was trying to dig Hal out." Oh, the hell of those few moments, when she didn't know if he was dead or alive.

"It was a mercy you were there. You were able to raise the alarm and help save Ansford."

Tia's heart thumped painfully. Had she—however inadvertently—brought about the entire catastrophe? Was she to blame? She fought to keep the wobble out of her voice as she asked, "What brought the building down? Was there an earthquake?"

"Lynch has sent for a surveyor to find out. Currently, he thinks the mortar may have failed. It could have been scoured out by the bad weather we had a few years ago, and frost might have weakened the masonry, making it spall and crack." Mama paused and shuddered melodramatically. "I didn't like that folly at all—it was eerie, and I never went near the place, as you well know. I do hope Ansford had nothing valuable in there, for everything's been reduced to dust."

"Do you think he'll rebuild it?" She hadn't meant to voice the thought aloud. Pondering Hal's monument to Mary, Tia prayed he wouldn't want to resurrect it.

"What an odd question to ask. Why, no. I believe Ansford declared—in a rather colorful fashion as they were cleaning him up—that he was relieved it was gone. It was as if the place had an unnatural hold on him."

Tia couldn't agree more. But was the hold now broken? Could she and Hal finally be free from Mary Pelham's unforgiving influence?

"Tia, you're so pale. Shall I fetch the basin?"

"Oh Mama, I fear it is all my fault." She wrenched back a sob.

"Don't be silly. How could it be?"

"Bessie," she choked out, "would you leave us for a moment, please?"

"Of course, miss." The girl bobbed respectfully and left.

Clasping her hands together, Tia discovered how sore they were. Every cut buzzed from the alum water, and the tips of her bruised fingers ached.

"Now, what's all this nonsense about the folly's collapse being your fault?" Mama asked softly.

"Oh Mama, Lord Ansford asked me to marry him."

Chapter 45

"Well. Goodness. Gracious." Mama fell silent a moment, regarding Tia anxiously. "But how could something as momentous as this come to pass and I not be aware of it? He always seemed so cold, so distant."

With a shake of her head, Mama rose from her seat beside Tia's bed and began a perambulation of the bedchamber. "He must have seen your value as a tutor to Polly, and how you get on with all the servants and thought you would make a good helpmate."

Tia would have laughed had she not been traumatized. "I like to think he hasn't been quite so calculating, Mama. He told me he loved me."

"Now I've heard everything." Mama spun back to face her. "I wasn't certain the man even had a heart anymore. Though he's been unbending more of late and coming out of his mourning clothes."

Thank goodness Mama didn't know exactly *how* much Hal had come out of his clothes.

"I wondered if that was all due to you. But it's most remiss of you not to tell me the way the wind was blowing."

"I hardly knew it myself," Tia countered. "I accepted him, but we quarreled in the folly, and I changed my mind."

How could she have been so rash? She loved him. She should have been prepared to wait for him to prove he loved her in return. Maybe this disaster could have been averted.

"When I ran out, he came after me and must have slammed the door behind him. I don't know—I was too distracted. One moment he was standing at the top of the steps and the next, they simply disintegrated. I thought I'd lost him. It would have been all my fault."

She could no longer hold back the tears. As the first painful sob burst free, Mama rushed forward and held out her arms. "Come, Tia, don't be ashamed. You're never too big for a mother's cosseting."

Sinking into her embrace, Tia gave vent to all the fear, guilt, and hysteria threatening to overwhelm her, sprung from the awful moment she believed the man she loved was dead.

After what seemed like hours, her tears lessened, and she became aware of a subtle tapping coming from the door to the adjoining room.

Hal. Who else could it be?

"Mama, I think I need to sleep now. Please go and take some rest yourself."

"Are you sure you'll be all right?"

"Quite sure. I'm so weary, I could slumber for a week. Thank you."

Mama stood. "Rest. I shall return with some palatable refreshment in an hour or so." She left the room.

Easing herself stiffly out of bed, Tia padded across to the door and put her ear to it, then whispered against the crack, "Hal, is it you?" Her heart thudded in her chest as she awaited the response and when it came, she almost sank to the floor in relief.

"Of course it is, foolish woman. Who else would it be? How is a man supposed to rest with all this ruckus coming from your room?"

Scarcely able to contain her joy, she turned the key and flung the door open.

Chapter 46

Hal couldn't blame Tia for the horrified look she shot him as he hobbled into the room, his ankles protesting painfully. He'd caught sight of himself in the mirror earlier and was reminded forcibly of some of the wounded veterans he'd seen begging in the streets in London. His torso was bandaged tightly, as was his head. One eye was reduced to a swollen, reddened slit, and his nose bled.

His heart had been bleeding too, forced to listen to Tia's sobs but unable to go to her. In the end, he'd decided propriety could go hang and he must access her bedchamber come heaven, hell, or high water.

Once he'd established Tia was alone, Hal wasted no time in settling himself on the bed beside her.

It was peculiar, seeing her tearstained face and dark curls in the bed where Mary used to sleep, but he thrust the memory away. Mary no longer mattered.

"Oh Hal, I was so worried! I thought I'd lost you."

He tried to smile, but his lips were so dry it felt more like a grimace. "*I* thought I'd lost me, too. But the doctor says I'll live—I'm merely somewhat fragile and have split my head."

It pained him like the blazes but he wasn't about to admit it. He'd broken some ribs as well. Doubtless, other hurts would come to light once the initial shock had passed.

"I didn't mean to disturb you. I'm so sorry. It all just sort of . . . came out."

He reached for her, then hesitated. "Are you badly injured?"

Mercifully, she shook her head. Still, he held her gently. How wonderful, to be able to touch another warm, vital human being. He'd spent too long in the half-light with a woman made of dead, cold stone.

"I only have a few cuts and bruises," Tia murmured against his chest. "I have no excuse for being such a watering pot."

"Nonsense." His voice was hoarse from the dust he'd inhaled, and it was an effort to hold back a coughing fit. "You've been very brave, my love. You dug me out of the rubble when other young ladies would have run off screaming or fainted. And I was only jesting when I complained you'd disturbed me. I was desperate for an excuse to come in and see you, but Symons has become a martinet and is following Dr. Simpson's instructions to the letter. Remind me never to be injured again—it gives the servants an excuse to turn into bullies."

She sank farther into his embrace, laying her cheek against his chest. He rested his chin atop her head, and they sat there in companionable silence for many minutes.

Gradually he became aware her shoulders were shaking. "Are you weeping again, my sweet?" He held her as tightly against his damaged ribcage as he dared.

"Only a little," came the muffled reply.

"I think rest is called for. And perhaps hot brandy and milk to help you sleep." But he couldn't leave her yet. There was something he needed to say.

She nestled closer. "I'm so foolish, getting all upset when it is you who are more badly hurt and in the most serious danger."

"I beg you, don't punish yourself. Would you believe me if I told you I never wanted to live more than in the moment the rubble buried me? After Mary's death, the bitterness I awoke in her, the guilt I felt for allowing it to happen, I wanted to die. Whenever I gazed down from the top of the folly, I fought an almost irresistible urge to jump. I've not had the compulsion lately, not even when you walked away from me and I feared I'd destroyed all my hopes by showing you the sculpture."

He shuddered at the memory. "When the folly began to collapse, I knew things couldn't end that way, that I didn't want release. I wanted another life, a new life, with you. So, I jumped."

"You jumped?"

"Yes. I leapt as far out as I could, to try and get clear of the masonry from the tower. I landed on the grass some distance away and thus avoided being buried too deeply. My ankles continue to protest the feat, but they've been splinted and will mend in time. It was a terrible moment, I can tell you. There was so much weight on my spine I thought it would break, and I never expected to be able to breathe again. My head hurt like the devil, and I was in total darkness, thinking I'd been struck blind. Then I heard your voice, calling me back into the light. I made a gargantuan effort at movement and caught your attention. If I hadn't had you to live for, I might have succumbed."

"What about Polly?"

He hadn't forgotten Polly. It was his duty to his child that had kept him going thus far, even though she reminded him of Mary, of the pain of losing his wife in such grim circumstances. "Children are resilient—she would have been well cared for if the folly had claimed me. And she would have had *you*."

"She needs you too, Hal. At this very moment, she's probably weeping in her room, desperate to see us and to know we're all right."

"Should I send for her?"

"You should. And you must make every effort to love her, be a true father to her. Promise me."

He *did* love his daughter. It was why he'd planned to protect her by giving her a strict upbringing. But Tia had shown him how shortsighted the idea was. "I promise you I will. Now, I shall ring for Bessie, so she can fetch you that milk and brandy. You must sleep, my love."

"And she must bring Polly too, even if only for a short while."

Hal squeezed his eyes tight shut. It was ignoble for a man to weep, even if they were tears of joy. He could scarce believe he'd not only found someone who cared for him but was ready to love his daughter, too.

Tia's hurts would mend. In time, his would as well, and as soon as they were both recovered, he would repeat his offer of marriage.

And he would most definitely *not* take 'no' for an answer.

Epilogue

On their wedding day, Tia had been delighted to find the church thronged with all the best local families, many of Hal's former colleagues, his relations, and old friends. The latter included the Duke and Duchess of Finchingfield, both glowing with happiness in expectation of the arrival of their second child.

If Hal had been worried about being shunned by Society due to the wicked rumors about his wife's death and his subsequent seclusion, it was plain he needn't have done so.

The presence of the Duke and Duchess had lent respectability to the gathering, giving Tia hope Hal would soon be welcomed back into political life—and would once again have a purpose—one involving the living rather than the dead.

It was now a full month since the wedding. October was nearly ended, and the trees had started to drop their golden cascade of leaves upon the ground. The passageways of Foxleaze were chill, but the bedchamber had a fire burning cheerfully in the grate.

Hal still slumbered. They'd retired early the previous evening, made love with vigorous enthusiasm, and hadn't fallen asleep until the first cock began to crow. Tia's rest had been fitful, however. She had a gift she wanted to present to him today—but her courage had begun to fail her, not knowing if it would be taken in the spirit in which it was intended. She had secretly commissioned the work when he was bedridden, recovering from his injuries.

Throwing a wrap over her nightgown, she slipped out of his bedchamber and made her way to his study. The room had a completely different aspect to it now, with the late baroness's portrait no longer hanging above the fireplace. Hal was already working on its replacement, in an attic he'd converted into a studio.

The old picture was to be substituted by a portrait of Tia. In fact, her husband was working on *two* portraits, but the first was for personal consumption only, depicting the new Baroness Ansford with her hair loose about her shoulders, wearing a low-necked muslin dress which clung to her curves in an almost indecent fashion.

The other painting he was creating was much more respectable. In that portrait, Tia was dressed in a smart riding habit, with a dashing hat and a pair of beige kid gloves in her hand. She glanced toward the viewer in three-quarter face, her expression both proud and benign.

She'd told him she could never appear so top-lofty, but he'd refused to make any changes. The portrait was destined for a new wing of the Selbury Poorhouse, being built with the joint patronage of her husband and the Duke of Finchingfield. It was to house the Lady Galatea Ansford School, where the young paupers would learn domestic skills, as well as their numbers and letters.

Hal had already generously donated some reference books from his library, prompting Polly to offer up some of her own illustrated storybooks. If he needed any proof Tia's loving and indulgent approach toward the child hadn't spoiled Polly, this was surely it.

Tia was, of course, delighted that her good fortune in marrying a wealthy and influential man meant she could help the pauper children she'd left behind. The new wing had been a sort of wedding present from her husband, and she'd told him—her eyes awash with tears of joy—that she could never have dreamed of a better one.

She wandered across to the study window and gazed out across the cloisters to the park beyond. Suddenly the door opened, but before she could turn around, she was grasped from behind and pulled up against a deliciously firm male body.

"Why did you get up?" His voice against her ear was a delicious purr. "Come back to bed."

She trembled in Hal's grasp as she felt the wonder of his growing arousal pressed against her bottom. His hands around her waist began to slide up toward her breasts, but she pushed them down. "Not now, Hal. We need to talk."

"Oh dear, that sounds ominous." Tia could hear the humor in Hal's tone. He kept his hands where they were but didn't release her.

"I can't believe it's actually gone." She glanced toward where the line of the treetops was no longer interrupted by the darkly brooding tower. All trace of the folly had vanished and with it the secrets of the past, the ghosts, and the grim memories.

With its loss, the eeriness of Foxleaze had departed as well. She knew the shadows of the cloisters held no specters, the family mausoleum no vengeful spirits, and the gargoyles and ceiling bosses were no longer demons turned to stone, awaiting the right touch of magic to bring them all tumbling back into the world again.

It was just as well, for as she was now mistress of this house, it wouldn't do to be afraid to walk the passageways at night.

"It's gone. And I don't miss it one iota. Not now I have you."

"It is a great pity your memorial sculpture of Mary should be lost. It was a stunning piece of work."

"I'm honored you should think so. I'm sad for Polly's sake I can no longer build the impressive monument to her mother I'd intended, but it can't be helped."

Tia turned around slowly and gazed up into Hal's eyes. "It's possible it can." She scanned his beloved face. Now the injuries caused by the fall of the folly had healed, he was more beautiful than ever. Especially when he regarded her with that particular expression, combining adoration and arousal.

But she was going to make him wait a little longer before he received what his body so clearly wanted. There were two hearts, two souls, needing resolution.

"Hal, I have a surprise for you. Can you dress quickly and come down to the cloisters with me?"

His mouth drooped. "Not what I had in mind." His tone was velvety soft and alluring.

"Hal, please." She used what she called her Schoolmistress Voice now. He and Polly were rapidly learning *never* to ignore it.

"Very well. But we'd best take coats—the cloisters get so draughty this time of year. Are you positive you don't want to wait until after breakfast?"

"Hal!"

"Oh, all right. I'll get dressed." He fell back to let her past him, and she experienced, as she always did, the lightning flash of awareness when their bodies were close, but not quite touching. Once she had given him her gift, breakfast would have to wait, while they attended to . . . other matters.

Tia slipped through the door into her own bedchamber. The bed was aired, as usual, the covers turned down, but it was quite clear it hadn't been slept in. What the servants must think of their new mistress, she daren't imagine. Who could have known she'd become a total wanton so early in her marriage? Her heart fluttered, and she was all fingers and thumbs as she struggled into her chemise and petticoats.

A front-fastening gown was necessary to attire herself without Hal's help, for if she went to him demanding to be laced up, they would face another delay before she revealed her surprise.

Would he like it? Would he hate it? Would he appreciate the reasoning behind her gift? A good deal was riding on whether or not she'd done the right thing.

A soft tap on the adjoining door signaled Hal was ready and moments later they descended hand-in-hand down the stone steps into the cloisters. She lit a lantern and led him into the crypt.

The shadows fled into the corners, where they congregated in the crisply cut lettering and marble drapes of the Pelham monuments. Resting atop the late baroness's flat marble tomb was an oddly-shaped object, swathed in sacking.

"Tia, what's this?" Hal wore a bemused frown.

She clasped her hands tightly together. "Take off the wrapping and see." It was a struggle to keep the anxiety from her voice.

He lifted the sacking and gasped. Was it a *good* gasp, or a bad one? She shifted from one foot to the other, living an eternity in a few seconds.

He turned to her, amazed. "You had it mended? When? How? And more importantly, why?"

Now revealed in all its glory, a plaster bust of the late Mary Pelham, complete with masterfully sculpted veil, stood at the head of her tomb.

As soon as Tia had been well enough to get out and about after the accident, she'd paid some of the local children, headed by Sammy, the gardener's boy, to sort through the rubble for any pieces of marble they could find. Once the heap was complete, she'd joined the children in the largest greenhouse, trying to find every single part of that broken, once-beautiful face.

It was possible the whole monument might have been reconstructed, but she wanted all evidence of their activities cleared away by the time Hal resurfaced and was able to walk about his grounds again, so she'd settled for the head and shoulders only.

With the assistance of her friend Lucy, Duchess of Finchingfield, whose husband was an expert on sculpture, Tia had been put in touch with a workshop where busts were produced, in both plaster and stone. Mary Pelham's effigy had been glued back together and a mold made of it, including a reinforced stand with a wide base so the bust could sit upon any flat surface. Next, a plaster cast had been created and faint veins of gray, echoing the original marble, had been painted on the surface.

The bust had been so expertly finished, no casual observer would have had any idea it was mere plaster. Nor would they have been aware the original had more adjoining pieces than dozens of children's jigsaw puzzles.

"I will tell you the when and the how shortly. As for the why, it's because your work was too masterful to lose. I wished you to have the monument you wanted—at least in part. I wanted to give Polly somewhere to come if she ever needed to confide in her mama's spirit. Most of all, I needed you to know it doesn't matter to me anymore how you feel about Mary. I promise not to be jealous—"

He interrupted her by sweeping her into his arms and kissing her so thoroughly, she feared she'd faint from joy. When he released her and looked down at her, his blue gaze was soft, his face shining with emotion.

Her heart swelled to bursting with her love for him.

"Thank you, Tia. It's a fitting memorial to Mary, and I would never have thought of making a gesture like that, selfish, shortsighted fool that I am. Let me assure you right now there's no longer any room in my heart for Mary. There is only you, and Polly, who utterly adores you. You have saved not one life, but two, Galatea Pelham, Lady Ansford, and I will thank you for it until my last breath. I promise never to neglect you in favor of any other business. I refuse to let you leave my side. Ever."

She was able to breathe again. Her gift had been a success. "Not even when you're painting in your studio?"

"No, for you will be sitting for me."

"Not even when you're giving a speech in Parliament?"

He grinned and stroked her waist, pulling her closer. "No, for you will be up in the gallery, listening."

"Not even when you're asleep?"

"Especially not then. For who would soothe me when I wake from the nightmare of Mary's fall, but you? Who would wrap around me to keep off the chill of autumn, if not you? Who would willingly give themselves to me, mind, soul and body, when I had need of them, but you? You are all the world to me, my love. Now and forever."

"Now and forever." Tia sent up a silent offer of thanks to the lingering spirit that had released him, finally, into her arms.

And into her heart.

CPSIA information can be obtained
at www.ICGtesting.com
Printed in the USA
LVHW081107230123
737753LV00014B/790